Praise for *Noopiming*

"How is it that Leanne Betasamosake Simpson's fiction can feel both familiar and warm like old teachings and absolutely fresh and brand new? Is it even fiction? *Noopiming* seems to exist somewhere in the in-between, with all the best parts of poetry and story. As always, I am in awe of Leanne Betasamosake Simpson, prolific in every way." — KATHERENA VERMETTE, bestselling author of *The Break* and *The Strangers*

"This imaginative book is what would happen if we gave pen and paper to the deepest, most secretive parts of ourselves. Down to the fibres, down to each breath, Leanne Betasamosake Simpson dares to explore not only the humanity of a character, but the humanity of the parts that make us whole, in a world running on empty." — CATHERINE HERNANDEZ, bestselling author of *Scarborough*

"*Noopiming* is a rare parcel of beauty and power, at once a creator and destroyer of forms. All of Simpson's myriad literary gifts shine here — her scalpel-sharp humour, her eye for the smallest human details, the prodigious scope of her imaginative and poetic generosity. The result is a book at once fierce, uproarious, heartbreaking, and, throughout and above all else, rooted in love." — OMAR EL AKKAD, Scotiabank Giller Prize–winning author of *What Strange Paradise*

"Leanne Betasamosake Simpson's *Noopiming* once again confirms her position as a brilliant, daring experimentalist and a beautiful, radical portraitist of contemporary NDN life. The prose hums with a lovingness that moved me to tears and with a humour that felt plucked right out of my rez adolescence. The chorus of thinkers, dreamers, revolutionaries, poets, and misfits that Simpson conjures here feels like a miracle. My heart ached and swelled for all of them. What I adored most about this book is that it has so little to do with the white gaze. Simpson writes for us, for NDNs, those made to make other kinds of beauty, to build other kinds of beautiful lives, where no one is looking. *Noopiming* is a book from the future! Simpson is our much-needed historian of the future!" — BILLY-RAY BELCOURT, award-winning author of *This Wound is a World* and *NDN Coping Mechanisms*

"I'm pretty sure we don't deserve Leanne Betasamosake Simpson. But miracles happen, and this is one. This book is poem, novel, prophecy, handbook, and side-eyed critique all at once. This book doesn't only present characters you will love and never want to leave (but yes, it does), it doesn't only transform the function of character and plot into a visibly collective dynamic energy field (and hallelujah), but it also cultivates *character* in the reader, that we might remember what we first knew. Which is that what seems separate was never separate. What feels impossible is already happening. And it depends on our most loving words. It requires our most loving actions towards each other. The ceremony has been found." — ALEXIS PAULINE GUMBS, author of *Dub: Finding Ceremony*

"This brilliant novel is a carefully curated mix of prose and poetry, though the narrative and poetic form never leaves either; at all times, there is a deliberate attention to rhythm, movement, and sound.

The layered storytelling is rich with wry and undeniable humour and introduces readers to an incredible cast of characters, giving us the perspective of Elders, Indigenous youth, raccoons, geese, and trees, braiding together past, present, and future and intentionally centring Nishnaabe life and practices . . . This is the beauty and masterful work of this novel: it holds something for every Indigenous person. It's a gift that feels specifically for us." — *Globe and Mail*

"[*Noopiming*] presses readers — Indigenous and settler alike — to consider the novel form as a wider venue for storytelling than it is traditionally conceived . . . Language is thrilling in all of Simpson's work, and nowhere more so than in this newest offering . . . Simpson's writing is at once political and loud, honest and whisper-quiet . . . This novel will be reread for its many truths and teachings and for its undeniable power. The complicated questions *Noopiming* poses are worth revisiting, and the novel's wisdom will continue to grow as the reader does." — *Quill & Quire*, STARRED REVIEW

"A piercing, original novel." — *Publishers Weekly*

"Taking traditional Anishinaabe teachings and weaving them through contemporary forms of understanding, Simpson brings the reader into not a new world, but a world already existing, one that breaks through the colonial bars that try to cage it." — *Rabble.ca*

Also by the Author

Fiction

This Accident of Being Lost
Islands of Decolonial Love: Stories & Songs
The Gift Is in the Making: Anishinaabeg Stories

Non-Fiction

*A Short History of the Blockade: Giant Beavers, Diplomacy,
and Regeneration in Nishnaabewin*
*As We Have Always Done: Indigenous Freedom
through Radical Resistance*
*Dancing on Our Turtle's Back: Stories of Nishnaabeg
Re-Creation, Resurgence, and a New Emergence*

Albums

Theory of Ice
f(l)ight
Islands of Decolonial Love

Anthologies

*The Winter We Danced: Voices from the Past, the Future, and the Idle
No More Movement* (Kino-nda-niimi Collective)
This Is an Honour Song: Twenty Years Since the Blockades
(edited with Kiera Ladner)
*Lighting the Eighth Fire: The Liberation, Resurgence, and Protection
of Indigenous Nations*

NOOPIMING

THE CURE FOR WHITE LADIES

LEANNE
BETASAMOSAKE SIMPSON

ANANSI

Published in Canada in 2020 by House of Anansi Press Inc.
www.houseofanansi.com

House of Anansi Press is committed to protecting our natural
environment. This book is made of material from well-managed
FSC®-certified forests, recycled materials, and other controlled sources.

House of Anansi Press is a Global Certified Accessible™ (GCA by
Benetech) publisher. The ebook version of this book meets stringent
accessibility standards and is available to students and readers with
print disabilities.

26 25 24 23 22   4 5 6 7 8

Library and Archives Canada Cataloguing in Publication

Title: Noopiming : the cure for white ladies / Leanne Betasamosake Simpson.
Names: Simpson, Leanne Betasamosake, 1971– author.
Identifiers: Canadiana (print) 20200208365 | Canadiana (ebook)
20200208373 | ISBN 9781487007645 (softcover) |
ISBN 9781487007652 (EPUB) |
ISBN 9781487007669 (Kindle)
Classification: LCC PS8637.I4865 N66 2020 | DDC C813/.6—dc23

Cover design: Alysia Shewchuk

*House of Anansi Press respectfully acknowledges that the land on which
we operate is the Traditional Territory of many Nations, including the
Anishinabeg, the Wendat, and the Haudenosaunee. It is also the Treaty
Lands of the Mississaugas of the Credit.*

*We acknowledge for their financial support of our publishing program
the Canada Council for the Arts, the Ontario Arts Council, and the
Government of Canada.*

Printed and bound in Canada

To my heart, the Michi Saagiig Nishnaabeg,
and to all of our anticolonial relations with whom
we share the big lake, and the world.

Counting her own theory, the theory of nothing, she had opened up the world.

— Dionne Brand, *A Map to the Door of No Return*

This is an aesthetics of turbulence whose corresponding ethics is not provided in advance.

— Édouard Glissant, *Poetics of Relation*

Anybody who thinks that they can understand how terrible the terror has been, without understanding how beautiful the beauty has been against the grain of the terror, is wrong.

— Fred Moten

NOOPIMING

ONE

SOLIDIFICATION

Once you move through cold, there is pacific.

Once you move through pacific, there is placid.

Once you move through placid, there is a condition of expanse.

And it was that condition of expanse that held me.

I heard them singing above me:

Mashkawaji fell through the ice
to find quiet
to get out of the wind
to visit with namegos

They all sang:

> *Mashkawaji stitches up the hole*
> *they are so cold they can't move*
> *they are frozen stiff*
> *the lake is their blanket*

They all sang:

Mashkawaji is frozen stiff
still
calm
no one knows if they're coming back

They all sang:

Akiwenzii is fishing through the ice with a spear
they brought a line of beads
they will wait patiently
they will wait until Mashkawaji is done their visit

The singing and drumming came every night, from a distance. Different choirs every evening at dusk, marking the passage of time, reminding me there is still love.

You see, tragedy happened again. The details don't matter because the details are hopeless, overwhelmed, shut down.

Know this: After two years, the best parts of me are still frozen in the lake — my limbic system; its best friend, the prefrontal cortex; and the hollow, pumping organ in which I keep benevolence. The only one that regularly comes to visit is Akiwenzii. In the winter they park their truck on the ice, drill a hole with the auger and fish until the cold makes their bones crack. As soon as the ice is off the lake, Akiwenzii is back in their boat, with a torch and a sort of pitchfork for spearing pickerel. In the dead of summer, Akiwenzii sneaks back before first light in their canoe, before the cottagers and their jet skis are out. In the fall, they sprinkle tobacco around me and sing.

My world is muted. I look out. If something upsets me, I just wait, and the upset passes. I sit beside. Sometimes, I remember the other me, before I was frozen in the lake. I remember caring and engaging and the sharpness of unmuted feeling. I remember hopeless connection.

I don't feel stuck, in part because I don't feel anything. Their song isn't wrong, the ice is like a warm, weighted blanket. My form dissolved when tragedy came and if I am fluid, the ice is container.

There are ashes in my eyes.

I am so far inside myself. Like miskwaadesi on a full fast inside time, pulled inside their organs, inside their turtle shell, inside the sediments of the lake, while the iceworld forms on top, oblivious to the outside with body as lake.

And there is solace in being cut off.

And there is freedom enmeshed within that state.

Know this: Being frozen in the lake is another kind of life.

Know this: It is unclear how long before I will be done with my visit. It is unclear how long visiting takes.

Know this: Visiting is more of a dance than an event.

Akiwenzii is my will.

Ninaatig is my lungs.

Mindimooyenh is my conscience.

Sabe is my marrow.

Adik is my nervous system.

Asin is my eyes and ears.

Lucy is my brain.

I believe everything these seven say because ice distorts perception, and trust replaces critique, examination and interrogation.

I believe everything these seven say

even though,
even though.

I believe everything these seven say
even though
their truths are their own,
not mine.

I believe: In the absence of my own heart,
I will accept the hearts of these seven.

The geese fly overhead in the sheer grace of a carefully angled formation designed to take them elsewhere.

There are still stars.

There are still stars.

TWO

AFFINITIES

MINDIMOOYENH

Mindimooyenh counts their steps in their head. Every day. All day long. They also make lists on scrap paper, cut coupons, shop all the grocery store chains by taking the bus, studying the flyers and buying only what is on special that week. All of their produce comes from the dead-vegetable bin, which is the place in the grocery store where rotten fruit and vegetables are packaged up and sold for a discount. Mindimooyenh calls the specials "bargoons." Nothing makes Mindimooyenh happier than a bargoon.

Mindimooyenh does their work alone, except when it is a "two per customer" situation. Then we all get dragged to wait in separate lines with baggies full of loonies.

One day Mindimooyenh finds a pair of ugly brown high-tech hiking boots on sale for $29.99 in the Mark's Brothers Work Wearhouse flyer.

I say, "It's just Mark's."

They say, "I know." So they take the bus to the store, but when they get there, the Mark's Brothers does not have their size in the $29.99 model, only the $32.99 model. Now, Mindimooyenh can afford the extra $3 easy. Instead, they get the $29.99 ones in a too-small size, because the sheer joy of the bargoon outweighs the pain of too-small shoes, and who do I think I am waltzing around the reserve with shoes that cost $32.99 anyway.

"I just shut my feet off when they hurt," they say.

Sometimes Sabe goes with Mindimooyenh, but Mindimooyenh is hard to keep up with and the nervous energy is jolting and exhausting.

Sabe has a tendency to show up at dramatic times and then disappear through the normal. Sabe thinks no one notices, because they don't *seem* to notice, but that's not true. It is just something Sabe tells themselves. Everyone notices when they are not there, which is most of the time.

Sabe makes a point of showing up at the sweats, and for Lucy's fasts. Sabe keeps an eye on Ninaatig. They usually run into Adik on the trail. They see Akiwenzii mostly in ceremony. Mindimooyenh is harder. Mindimooyenh is always moving around, busy, and to be honest, Sabe doesn't like the run-ins with them anyway. They tend to be a harsh mirror of things Sabe doesn't particularly like about themselves.

Sabe has been sober for over a year now. Completely sober, as in no drinks and no funny business, not just an absence of inebriation. It was not necessarily a struggle to stop. They are calmer now and they can sleep through the whole night. They can eat cake because their beer gut vanished. Their serotonin levels are up so they are not depressed and anxious all the time. They have a lot more time on their hands. They are relearning things like fun and happy and how to talk basic-human with basic humans about nothing.

The only real downside is that Sabe spends more time alone and more time in their head than before. They have less patience for people. They have to find benevolence in different places and then really focus and sort of lie, collecting it up and storing it in their hiding spot.

Sabe remembers how the first sip of beer used to bring relief. An escape from the tightness of muscles wound around their frame. They remember how words would flow out of their mouth like exhalations, one after another, and everything was easier than it should've been. Laughing was easy. They remember how it felt subversive, NDN, rebellious without the rebellion. They remember how sitting in a bar with Lucy was like a revolution without the revolution.

They remember the wave of effortless happy. The false comradery. The illusion of easy intimacy without the intimate. The shame spiral of the morning after.

They remember the precise moment the night would turn, and things would get said that were usually not said. Things would get done that were usually not done. The boundaries that would be crossed and how the ideas that floated around in the back of their head and normally carried no importance became life and death. They remember that as fear.

Sabe doesn't remember the precise moment casual indifference, or mild like even, turned to intense hatred. It was like something snapped in them. They remember where: Dawson City. They remember when: June 21. They remember being with Lucy and Asin, who were already sober. They remember the details of circumstance. But none of the whys add up.

It doesn't take an enormous amount of self-awareness to see the irrationality of the decision, but it also doesn't take an enormous amount of self-awareness to see it as a reasonable one. What concerns Sabe is that they thought about it before, lots of times, and they always decided they wanted to take a more measured response. Some Ancestors drink. Some Spirits drink. It gives them empathy and understanding for the humans that do. Everything is fucked up. Everyone is fucked up. Even the Ancestors and the Spirits. No one likes a goddamn judge.

And then one day, Sabe woke up sure, and they've never been sure about anything before, not even about decisions that require certainty, but this time, they are certain. Even when they are in bars. Even when they are sad and in bars and surrounded.

It is Sabe's way of saying no. This is not right.

It just isn't.

And the truth is, in private, Sabe is judgy, because the damage is laid out and networked and it is inescapable. Once you can see the map of hurt, and how hurt gives birth to more hurt, the shallow justifications fall short. The politics smother. Akiwenzii saw it four decades sooner than Sabe, but at least Sabe saw it, right?

Sabe is sitting on their porch watching the birds at the feeder. There is a baby grackle yelling at its parent because it wants birdseed. The parent grackle is hurrying up to the feeder, they get the seeds, chew the seeds and put them in baby's mouth. Over and over. Baby grackle just yells at parent grackle. The tenderness is gone, only relentless irritation remains, and staying becomes another word for love.

Sabe is thinking about this in the context of their own life and then projecting their ideas onto the grackles. The parenting of humans is relentless. The continuous infusion of unconditional love. The patience in the face of the same mistakes over and over. The patience with the constant need for attention. With the narcissism. It's why Sabe retreats here. To the bush. To the cabin with the bird feeders and endless supply of seed. The humans think Sabe is off doing something important, and they are, just not in the way that would satisfy human expectation.

Things seem pretty fucked for the humans, to be honest. The white ones who think they are the only ones have really structured the fucked-up-ed-ness in a seemingly impenetrable way this time. A few good ones get their footing, and then without continual cheerleading, succumb to the shit talk. It is difficult to know where to intervene or how to start. There are embers, but the wood is always wet and the flames go out so damn easy.

Everyone thinks the Ancestors have all the answers, but sometimes, most times, it takes more.

SABE

Sabe keeps their special things wrapped in red cloth safety-pinned to their undershirt:

tiny piece of flat cedar

single strand of sweetgrass

pinch of tobacco

Akiwenzii lives on the reserve in a cabin they built for themselves. It is beside the dump, but it is a good-sized piece of land with places for ceremony and sugar-making and the trees are friendly. They have another cabin in the northern part of the treaty area for hunting, and this is really where Akiwenzii is at their best. Sometimes we go there to think.

Mostly Akiwenzii is real quiet when we go there. Just sits there looking bored, and not saying much. They get bored in town and even in the cabin, where basic life chores don't take up much time. Akiwenzii is better out in the bush in a tent. Get water. Make fire. Boil tea. Get spruce gum. Get ducks. Pluck ducks. Cook ducks. Cut wood. Get water. Make fire. Boil tea.

They get up real early. At dawn. Start the routine. Make fire. Boil tea. If you get up real early too, they'll tell you to work hard all day long. Go to bed when it gets dark. Get up when it gets light. They'll tell you to make sure there is a big pile of wood and kindling beside the cooking fire for the morning. "That's what the old people say," they say. Like they aren't an old person.

This morning, we're drinking tea and boiling eggs. Akiwenzii is going on and on about making medicine out of Windex to cure cancer. "Two parts Windex, four parts water, add the mashkiki and let it sit overnight. Drink like tea. One cup a day. Cleans you right out. Right out. That's it. Cancer over."

They are watching my reaction, I suspect to the Windex part. I'm acting like I fully believe them. Of course Windex could cure cancer. Of course. I mean, why not? Who knows the synergistic possibilities of Windex, water and bush medicine? I nod, smiling like a child, absorbing this new knowledge like a sponge, imagining spraying Windex on my bruises, hangnails, and face for a more youthful complexion. I imagine spraying it on my kid's cuts like a loving parent would spray on Polysporin before the SpongeBob Band-Aid.

Every afternoon they are out getting spruce gum with their axe and a Ziploc baggie. They must have ten bags full by now and I wonder what they are going to do with all of it. I go out with them too, but I feel bad for the trees. The only trees that have big clumps of spruce gum are injured trees. The new spruce gum is like tears, or maybe blood, and the dried stuff is like a scab. We're literally picking the scabs off of the tree's wounds. I tell this to Akiwenzii and they look at me with a smirk, like maybe I'm pulling their leg. Like this cannot possibly be how I really think. Then they shake their head and keep picking.

Sabe stops by for dinner and the two boil a moose head, teeth and all.

After I'm done the dinner dishes, Akiwenzii gets their Dr-Ho's Circulation Promoter out and hooks it up to their bare feet in front of the fire. They keep it in the original box, with the "As Seen on TV" sticker on the front. I see they have thirty-eight AAA batteries in the outside pocket of their duffle bag. Sometimes Sabe takes a turn too.

In December of every year, Mindimooyenh wanders through Ikea in North York each day, meditating like it is a labyrinth. They repeat "Gersby," followed by "Hemnes," over and over between the hours of 10 a.m. and 9 p.m. every day. They don't eat or drink except for $1.99 Ikea meatballs at 8:30 p.m., just before closing. Mindimooyenh takes the bus there and the bus home. They smudge in the parking lot before they go in. They put down their semaa in the *Ficus elastica* plant in the warehouse section.

Mindimooyenh is sitting on a lawn chair on the ice visiting me, talking and talking. It doesn't matter if you listen or pay attention or respond or talk to them back. And sometimes I like when they come around because it doesn't matter if I talk, not even one little bit. It doesn't even matter if I pay attention, because my response is irrelevant. Mindimooyenh is like that. Maybe because all those years in residential school they weren't allowed to talk, and now their words have just built up and come bursting out.

They are talking about sleeping in cars because they are scared of bears and it wouldn't be the first time they slept in a car and it won't be the last time. They are talking about babysitting three grandbabies and feeding and changing them and getting them all organized in an assembly line so no one is crying. They are talking about Numbnuts and at first I forget who he is, but as they go on I remember and he better hope they never run into him again.

They are talking about cooking roasts and turkeys for the feast in eight different slow cookers in the basement apartment where they stay and they hope they don't blow a fuse. They are talking about fans from the dollar store. They are talking about saving $100 worth of petunias from their daughter-in-law's garden. They are talking about all the bargoons they got at the auction with Akiwenzii.

Akiwenzii is just back from the auction. Their truck has a life-size plastic Santa Claus in the back, three more cast-iron frying pans and a large spool of "Pioneer Bailer Twine." I ask what that bailer twine is for and they say it's for me to make sweat lodges. There is enough for the next seven generations to make sweat lodges and the smell of mould hits me as I take the spool out of the truck. I ask what the five-foot-tall faded Santa is for. They say "target practice" and add "because you have the worst aim of anyone I've ever tried to teach." I do not ask about the frying pans.

Akiwenzii's house is bordering on *Hoarders*. Tobacco pouches and ties overflow birchbark baskets at the door. Water bottles and coffee mugs with various institutional logos; a pile of "Native art" prints in cellophane, each bought for prices ranging from $10 to $50. A mound of reusable tote bags, again with various institutional logos, spills out of a kitchen drawer. I can see these are gifts from speaking engagements and workshops. I can see the problem with institutional gifts.

MINDIMOOYENH

Mindimooyenh saves things too. Long toothpicks from hors d'oeuvres from the fancy museum reception (for their hair), fishing line for when the arms break off their red dollar-store reading glasses, one-litre milk bags for sandwiches, paper placemats from the diner so their grandkids have something to colour on.

NINAATIG

Akiwenzii is sitting at the base bottom of Ninaatig watching the Tour de France on their phone. If you were to ask them, Akiwenzii would tell you that they and the tree are watching it together and maybe that is true. There is a love between these two.

I ask Akiwenzii why the Tour and why the tree.

They answer, "Because it is funny."

"Why?"

"Because of the way the announcer says "cobbles." Because these are a bunch of white men racing around with metal contraptions between their legs, for no reason. Because Ninaatig wants to know what is going on in the world. Because Ninaatig likes that they get up after the crashes. Trees can't do that."

Akiwenzii says that old trees like Ninaatig can suck the sad out of you and heal you if you hug them. Heal you meaning take the edge off, I think. I ask about consent.

"I would hate it if I was stuck in the ground and people just came up to me and hugged me without asking, demanding I suck the hurt out of them."

Akiwenzii shakes their head.

"Ninaatig only sucks if they want to. They don't suck for everyone. And what makes you think Ninaatig is stuck?"

NINAATIG

Ninaatig is Akiwenzii's oldest friend. They have been hanging out long before watching the Tour de France was a thing. Akiwenzii met Ninaatig as a toddler. They were wandering around in the bush one day and Akiwenzii was just drawn to Ninaatig. Every time their parents took them for a walk, the toddler sought out Ninaatig like other kids seek out candy. That's how it was for all of Akiwenzii's life. They just sought Ninaatig out. They just kept on visiting. Through the teen years, the band years, the poet years, the Chief years, the break-up years and now the old-age years. They just keep on visiting. Akiwenzii brings Mindimooyenh to visit Ninaatig more than once, but it never clicks for them. Mindimooyenh can't relax into the connection, and although Ninaatig tries, these things can't be forced.

Last year, Mindimooyenh had a job at the university advising the big shots on how to appear to change things without changing a single thing. But of course Mindimooyenh advised too much, in an un-reconciliatory tone, and of course they got fired. Not before they got four months' worth of zhoon though. Not before they got free chiropractor though. Not before they slapped the head of the C-list NDN academic department in the face for "being a sell-out prick" though.

This year, Mindimooyenh is working for themselves.

MINDIMOOYENH

Mindimooyenh is on the phone with Indian Affairs because they are paying for Kookum's goddamn new glasses come hell or high water.

MINDIMOOYENH

Mindimooyenh says: "You better figure out how to solve problems."

MINDIMOOYENH

Mindimooyenh says: "If you don't take care of your hurt, it comes out big when the shit hits the fan."

MINDIMOOYENH

Mindimooyenh says: "Stop fiddle-farting around, you're not building a pig barn."

MINDIMOOYENH

Mindimooyenh says: "Your hair looks like a hen's ass in a windstorm."

MINDIMOOYENH

Mindimooyenh says: "'I love you' is just words."

MINDIMOOYENH

Mindimooyenh says: "Grief is saving yourself over and over again."

MINDIMOOYENH

Mindimooyenh says: "We live in an ecosystem of hurt."

MINDIMOOYENH

Mindimooyenh is stockpiling. Not just bargoons, either. They are stockpiling the morning-after pill, the abortion pill and regular old condoms. Mindimooyenh buys their drugs online from an abortion pill website in the States and ships them to their postal box in Buffalo. Once a month or so, they shuffle off to Buffalo in their beater van and pick up the orders along with the other shit people want from American Walmart: Rogaine, cooking spray, fake butter. They stay in the van in the parking lot for three days because duty.

You can go to Mindimooyenh for the pills if you are in need, but there are criteria, unless you are Black, or NDN. Then that's all the criteria you need.

They cannot sleep here because every time ICE rips another family apart, their body produces slightly less melatonin because there is slightly less light, even though it is no different north of the medicine line.

Mindimooyenh dresses and talks and looks you in the eye just like a white lady to get back over the border. Sunglasses and everything.

ASIN

Asin and I talk about the same things each time: the death of satire, how we didn't predict things would get so bad, about the race to victimhood, identity politics, trauma-informed everything.

There are two parts to Asin. The defence and the heart: don't get tripped up by the defence.

Lucy and Asin are making this secret thing that no one else knows about. For the past few years, they get together — in restaurants, at each other's apartments, in Tommy Thompson park at night — and they work on it, one stitch at a time, one stitch after another.

Lucy is not good at sewing or precision and the project with Asin requires both. That's why Asin is there. They watched the YouTube video on how to do it, they invested in the correct tools including very expensive scissors that are not for paper, and they keep a careful watch over Lucy. Lucy's job is to make it happen. To keep the project progressing. To keep Asin on track. That part, they can handle. Lucy may not know how to make shit look good, but they do know how to get shit done.

Asin is good at making things look nice and so, at the beginning of the project, Lucy made Asin in charge of the materials. Asin spent a lot of time in Fabricland, even though that place is no Nishnaabe's favourite place to spend time in because it is nearly impossible to get out of there with black, red, yellow and white broadcloth without someone questioning you about your project, and don't even try with the Status card.

Asin signed up for the Fabricland Sewciety members' card to get the discount, and tried to think strategically about colour. If you arrange the colour in a particular way, the star will look like it is pulsing, but that might be placing the blanket bar too high for first-timers. Asin thought maybe they should try to make it so it wasn't an eyesore, but decided against yellows, oranges and reds and opted for blues, purples and reds.

Lucy waited outside.

LUCY

Lucy has a tendency to disappear and this is the most irritating thing to Asin. It's more than a tendency. Once a month, sometimes more. Asin gets mad every time. Lucy explains, promises to try harder. To be more open and present and forthcoming. And then, before Asin knows it, Lucy exits again. Lucy tries to explain that they always come back, but that's not nearly good enough for Asin. Asin always gets depressed and hopeless when Lucy leaves. Always.

LUCY

Lucy doesn't have a lot of time for depressed and hopeless. When they don't eat or drink like the old days. But they aren't in a lodge. They aren't surrounded by singers every night. They aren't supported by any old ones, except for Mindimooyenh, and I'm not sure you could call Mindimooyenh's presence support. At least not in the modern sense of the word. They are sometimes present, though — infrequently, but sometimes.

Lucy is in a tarp, hastily slung over some saplings and held down with rocks. They have a fire and a ring of cedar for protection. They have sweetgrass.

Lucy goes to the bush like this primarily to sleep and get away from their phone. The mouldy foamy and damp sleeping bag is the only place they can sleep for more than two hours in a row. And sleep means dream.

LUCY

When Lucy is trapped in the city they continuously stream episodes of *Star Trek* on Netflix to get through the night. They work their way through *The Next Generation, Voyager, Deep Space Nine, Enterprise* and the new one with all the queers. They go back over *The Next Generation* and *Voyager,* watching only the first few minutes of each episode. Lucy researches this practice because everyone knows that screens are bad for sleep. It feels like the sound occupies some part of Lucy's brain, the one responsible for the hamster wheel of thought, and allows everything else to shut off. This is Lucy's theory. It's unproven. Except that it's the only way they can sleep, even if it's only incrementally.

Lucy thinks of Tuvok and Chakotay as their best friends but Lucy keeps this to themselves.

ASIN

Asin does not disappear. They are constant. They will always answer texts and phone calls. Even in the bush. They believe in showing up.

ASIN

Asin is watching a YouTube video of a campfire, trying to fall asleep. Their second-floor apartment in the core is apocalyptically hot and this is the fourth day of the third heat emergency of the summer. Asin thinks they should really invest in air conditioning even though the $200 would stay on the credit card indefinitely. It's the subway ride home from Canadian Tire that would suck.

Lucy spends a lot of time trying to lure Asin out of the city on the GO train or the Greyhound. Asin always sounds interested, excited even, when Lucy brings it up, and the closer the date gets, the more over-whelming the thought of leaving the city is, and even if a physical ail-ment doesn't arise to prevent the detachment, an emotional one does and the plan falls through. Asin needs a lot of help to get moving, a lot of help to move outside of themselves. Although Lucy suspects that once in motion, the energy would be huge.

Akiwenzii tells both Lucy and Asin in no uncertain terms, "You need to sweat. Every month." Right now they manage to get their act together twice a year and that's it. It's not enough, Akiwenzii thinks. They need more practice. They need to be better at this before I go.

Lucy at least fasts, or Akiwenzii thinks they do. They come to the back of the property for four days every month and Akiwenzii doesn't know exactly what goes on back there, but rather than investigate, Akiwenzii makes the set of assumptions that makes them feel best and they don't dig any further.

Asin is in their thirties and under the impression they have lots of time to learn, and lots of time to change. Neither is true, but the illusion is real. Akiwenzii is trying to teach Lucy and Asin how to do ceremony, but it is going so much slower than they expected and they are having to relax their expectations. Maybe all the praying won't be in Nishnaabemowin. Maybe they will have to sing the same four songs every single time. Maybe they won't have much power because fasting the old way every year is too out of reach for this generation. Maybe each generation is just a watered-down version of the last. Akiwenzii stops this kind of thinking when they are in Asin's presence. It is not their place to think like this. There's also a small chance it's not true.

Asin spends as much time as possible in Tommy Thompson Park. The park is located on the Leslie Street Spit, a white man–made peninsula, and it is the only white man–made structure in the city that Asin enjoys. This doesn't mean it was or is a good idea to go there. Using the park is a compromise. No, that's not right. It is a place where birds congregate because there is no other place left. There are more than three hundred species there and so it is well known by ornithologists and birdwatchers, and in the fall and spring the migrating songbirds and shore birds stop on their way to something better. In this way, it reminds Asin of a campground along the Trans-Canada Highway in the prairies. Only for birds.

In the winter, Asin watches the boreal owl hunt for voles at dusk, and then Asin rides back to their apartment. The boreal owl is antisocial and nocturnal, like Asin. They are a sit-and-wait predator the size of a robin. They sit fifteen to twenty feet above the ground in trees, close to the trunk. The summer is their breeding season. While there are considerably fewer species of birds than there used to be, birds are still engaged in the building blocks of their nation, and they work to reproduce not just their bodies, but all the structures, behaviours and beliefs that enable large-scale survival. There are large-ish colonies of double-crested cormorants and black-crowned night-herons.

Asin does not have a life list of birds they have seen, because unlike most other birders, that's not why Asin is here.

Not everything is in fine working order on Akiwenzii's body any-more. They are returning to the earth in a slow, letting-go process. They are being pulled out of body and are sinking further into the universe.

I don't like it.

Akiwenzii finds it humiliating at the best of times.

It is an ugly process and there is no use romanticizing about it.

Akiwenzii used to run the sweats and that's the way Lucy liked it. All they had to do was show up and firekeep. This was the routine for several years, until Asin started showing up and firekeeping too and soon there were too many firekeepers and not enough bodies on the inside of the lodge. Akiwenzii took care of that. They told Lucy to come in and sit in the northern doorway.

Lucy didn't realize it at the time, which seems to be a key strategy with the Nishnaabeg, but any good firekeeper needs to know the intricacies of not just fire, but also water. If one doesn't know how those two work together, in sadness, in joy, in uncertainty and in hurt, then one can't sit where Akiwenzii sits. If one doesn't know how to work with heat and wet in the dry of winter or the humid of summer, the whole thing falls apart rather dramatically.

Akiwenzii comes in the lodge with one Ancestor, smokes their pipe and then leaves before the heat. They are sad when they leave, but they also don't want to have a heart attack in the lodge.

MINDIMOOYENH

Mindimooyenh says: "Ceremony is not an Instagram photo."

MINDIMOOYENH

Mindimooyenh says: "If it is a performance, the spirits refuse to show up. You guys are so full of shit you don't even notice."

MINDIMOOYENH

Mindimooyenh says: "We spend most of our time taking down our own."

MINDIMOOYENH

Mindimooyenh says: "Pay attention to the moon."

AKIWENZII

Akiwenzii is looking for a partner. A life partner, even though they don't have much life left. They tell me this is an impossible task, because things don't look good or work good and everyone is already dead.

I ask them what they want a partner for anyway.

They shake their head.

AKIWENZII

Akiwenzii is tired. Tired of acting like they are too old to be scared. Tired of acting like they are too old to care what they look like. Tired of acting like life experience has made them wise. Tired of being positive and having faith in the young people. Tired of the way what is most dear to them gets deployed and misused and performed. Tired of putting a happy goddamn spin on the end of the world.

I tell Akiwenzii that all the stories have been told. That there are no new ideas. You can try and make something up but chances are, it's already happened or it just doesn't matter. That we are stuck and anything that gets us unstuck seems trite.

"So?" they say.

"All the stories have always already been told. You just tell the same ones over and over and over and over and eventually, if you are patient, something you forgot breaks through. You aren't patient."

AKIWENZII

Akiwenzii keeps their special things in the glove compartment of their truck:

    claw of an eagle wrapped in red cloth

    flint and steel

    hunting knife

Akiwenzii and Mindimooyenh grew up together. Mindimooyenh is a little younger, but that doesn't stop them from telling Akiwenzii exactly what they think and it never has. They don't spend much deliberate time together now but proximity keeps them in contact on a weekly basis. This week, for instance, Mindimooyenh was tarp shopping at Canadian Tire and Akiwenzii was there in the lawn mower section looking at weed whackers because they were on sale. Mindimooyenh walked by pushing their cart full of Certified Value Tarps 15 × 20 in royal blue and said, "Birdseed is on sale, chum." Part of Akiwenzii felt irritated and part of Akiwenzii felt grateful for the reminder, because that was the item they'd come to Canadian Tire for in the first place.

Mindimooyenh is always waiting for the tarps to go on sale at Canadian Tire. They like the Certified Value Tarp 15 × 20 in royal blue, which is regularly $24.99, but currently the Certified Value Tarp 9 × 12 in green is on sale for $5.79 from $7.98. The last few years the polyethylene tarpaulin market has gone insane with sizing, colour and weave. Mindimooyenh will not be fooled by such trickery. They put twenty 15 × 20 blue tarps in their cart and pay with old-school Canadian Tire Money with a tax rebate for their Status card. Mindimooyenh gives the lineup they created the finger on the way out because they will be making things count right up until the very end.

Tarp as tent. Tarp as sleeping bag. Tarp as blanket.

MINDIMOOYENH

Nothing drives Mindimooyenh more crazy than "self-care."

"We are self-caring our way to fascism," they yell.

I try and explain.

"That's not a thing," they reply. "It is just care."

MINDIMOOYENH

Mindimooyenh says:

"Write a book! Win a prize!"

"Make a record! Win a prize!"

"Lake still smells like piss."

AKIWENZII

Akiwenzii says: "Trees are good because they are simultaneously networked into the sky, the dirt and the breath. They feel everything and they record it in their tree bones."

It has been a long time now since Ninaatig participated in the sugar-making ceremony by getting pierced. The piercings usually take place in the very first part of spring, when things are starting to melt and even the bush is sloppy. The ceremony lasts a full month at least, although now it is sometimes even longer with all the stopping and starting of climate change.

It was a useful ceremony for Ninaatig when they were young. It required focus and commitment. It required a luxurious reliance on Ninaatig's friends and neighbours, who were not pierced but were supporters. They made sure Ninaatig stayed hydrated by taking less water out of the soil. They caressed Ninaatig's skin during the drilling. They whispered beautiful things when the sun made the sap flow hard.

By midsummer, the wounds were mostly healed, and Ninaatig would be fully leafed and enjoying the humidity with their comrades. To be honest, Ninaatig missed the ceremony and the flow of the year, but no one tapped in the Mark S. Burnham Park because of the tree cops — though Ninaatig always knew it was on Lucy's mind. And by most accounts, Ninaatig's responsibilities in the world had shifted. The piercing had prepared them for their work now. The long hours, the travel, the pushing of the shopping cart until their branches ached.

THREE

OPACITY

NINAATIG

Ninaatig keeps their belongings in a shopping cart when they travel. Sabe repeatedly suggests that they use a suitcase with wheels, the kind that fits into an overhead bin on an airplane, and they even bring one from the dump beside Akiwenzii's for Ninaatig to try, but Ninaatig likes the shopping cart and it's never going into an overhead bin anyway.

Some like to pull. Others like to push.

One of Ninaatig's belongings is a copy of *The Hidden Life of Trees: What They Feel, How They Communicate — Discoveries from a Secret World*. They like to read broadly and particularly to have a measure of where human thinking is on them, so they know what is coming next.

Akiwenzii finds the book hilarious and offensive and they read it aloud and substitute the word "Indians" for trees: *The Hidden Life of Indians: What They Feel, How They Communicate — Discoveries from a Secret World*. They both laugh, although it hits a little too close to home.

Ninaatig also keeps a mason jar of soil in their shopping cart, for the times when they are surrounded by concrete and they can't find any. It is not enough to provide nutrients, but it is enough to provide emotional comfort, which is a fact too complex for *The Hidden Life of Trees*.

Perhaps the strangest thing Ninaatig has in their shopping cart is a leaf press. Ninaatig has had it for over fifty years. Someone left it in the bush at Ninaatig's base and when the person didn't come back for it, Ninaatig eventually emptied it out and put it in their shopping cart. Each year since, in the fall, Ninaatig picks one of their leaves like a poem and presses it. Their leaves are arranged in chronological order, one per year. At first, Ninaatig tried to remember the year, but after a decade or so time started to shift and meld together; some took on more prominence than others and some simply melted away altogether.

As the leaves dried, they lost their vitality and brightness, something Ninaatig regrets. The other trees didn't fully understand the leaf press, because they already recorded events in their bones, and these records didn't shift or meld. They didn't say anything.

NINAATIG

Ninaatig keeps their special things under their Certified Value blue tarp gifted from Mindimooyenh, and in their shopping cart:

The Hidden Life of Trees

leaf press

jar of soil

Whenever Ninaatig returns to the Mark S. Burnham forest, it is a joyous occasion. Ninaatig's children, grandchildren and great-grandchildren feel Ninaatig's absence, although they have come to live with it as a necessary, if unpleasant, part of life. Ninaatig too feels a sort of unrestricted joy being back amongst their closest people. Ninaatigoog always save Ninaatig's spot. Ninaatig can feel them moving their roots out of the ways as they stretch into the soil so that Ninaatig is grounded and hydrated. Ninaatig longs for the gentle sway of everyone's branches in unison when noodin shows up. They long for the nests and the visits from the birds, sometimes short, sometimes long. They maybe even long for baapaase. Maybe. They are in love with the harmony of the root nation. They are in love with Ninaatigoog.

And it feels good to not have to push the shopping cart around for a while. It needs better wheels, for one thing.

Ninaatig spends the winter sleeping in Mark S. Burnham Park. In the summer, Ninaatig travels around, visiting. Mostly goes to the city to see Adik, on the right side of Rosedale Valley Road, or to the reserve to see Akiwenzii, and they mostly run into Sabe on those trails between the city and the bush. There are only forty hectares of trees left in this park, and mostly things have been fine, but more recently the tree cops have taken an interest in "managing" the forest. That means new bathrooms, new signs, charging a ransom to hike the trail, and pruning. Ninaatig mostly ignores all this, but that doesn't mean it isn't irritating.

Adik and Ninaatig have been friends for centuries. Adik has changed over the years, though, that's for sure. They are hardened now, and more withdrawn — more lone wolf, albeit caribou-style.

Ninaatig knows why, but they can't think of a single thing to make it better.

Sabe is riding their bike around looking for Adik and going through people's recycling to weed out the good stuff. They have a shitty bike. A grey Supercycle from Canadian Tire, with curly handlebars and ten speeds from a time when ten speeds were more than enough speeds to traverse the landscape. The bike has a kickstand and fenders, which are essential accessories as far as Sabe is concerned, the seat cranked up high for Sabe's long legs and a rat trap perched on top of the back fender. Sabe has also attached an old kid's trailer that they found at the dump, to put the recycling in.

For a while Sabe collected old toilets and sinks from rich neighbourhoods and they would set them up in random places on the reserve. At the beach. In old Amos's backyard. In the field. In the sugar bush. It started off as a joke, but then some university students thought they saw deeper meaning to it and wrote about it for the school newspaper and before you knew it hordes of people were visiting to take photos.

Then someone hooked a sink up to one of the springs so water would pour out of it endlessly and people started using the toilets and one night, Sabe collected everything up and took it to the dump, in their bike trailer, one piece at a time.

Now they collect three things — bottles and cans for the refund, small appliances that can be fixed, and 250-ml plastic water bottles. The plastic water bottles are outside of their cabin on the reserve under a 30 × 60 Certified Standard Duty blue tarp in Large, $149.99 if you bought it new from aisle twenty-eight at Canadian Tire. The tarp smells like cat pee and Sabe found it in a blue bin in the Avenues. As if you can recycle polyethylene.

ADIK

Adik spends a lot of time with the Nishnaabeg and their friends in the fragment of bush on the right side of Rosedale Valley Road. Unlike Ninaatig, Adik avoids the side with the cemetery. No longer being in physical form has its emotional limitations and graveyards are one of them.

The Nishnaabeg have a few white-people tents and sleeping bags given to them by street outreach workers and if they need zhoon, the bottom of Rosedale Valley Road isn't the worst spot to ask for it. Mindimooyenh comes by every once in a while and leaves a pile of Certified Value Tarps 15 × 20 in royal blue for whoever needs one. There is also a weird lodge sculpture made out of hundreds of single-serving plastic water bottles. This is Sabe's crafty work since they have been sober and they are damn proud of it. It is the first of many projects, they think. Sometimes in a pinch, if someone new shows up without shelter, the Nishnaabeg throw one of Mindimooyenh's tarps over the plastic water bottle sculpture and call it "the Airbnb."

Mostly the place is quiet during the day, and the Nishnaabeg just show up at night to catch a few hours of uninterrupted sleep.

ADIK

Adik hangs out on the right side of Rosedale Valley Road for a different reason than Ninaatig. Adik thinks it's the only spot where hope lives, and they take out their voice recorder and record the sound of hope. It sounds like green leaves, attached to branches, moving in the wind.

ADIK

Sometimes Adik goes down the road into the valley late at night to drink from the Don River. It's not always worth it because of the anxiety it takes to get there. But on certain nights, the ones you can't predict, the taste of tires and gas moves to the background and Adik can only taste cool.

Every single time Ninaatig runs into Sabe it is magnificent. It is almost always on the path between the city and the reserve. It is always unexpected, and the connection is always immediate and like no time has passed. When Ninaatig and Sabe are together, they are the only world that exists. The light.

It is the same ceremony every time. They build a fire. They weave mats out of cattails to lie on. An effortless conversation is built around them and through them, and it seems like the more they share the more there is to share. At some point, their hearts feel very light, like they are leaving their bodies and dancing around the fire all on their own. They fall asleep holding each other.

Sabe wakes up feeling new, with an energy pulsing through them, and this makes the baamaa apii easier. But not easy.

Ninaatig watches Sabe walk down the path, north, through the oldest pines, full of sap. ·

SABE

Sabe knows that they should be visiting with Lucy because there is only one more night left and if they don't go tonight they'll have to wait until next month. They don't want to run into that damn Mindimooyenh, though. They can feel their anxiety marching through the bush thirty feet ahead of them.

Mindimooyenh is waiting at the front doors of Robarts Library at the University of Toronto and the sign says it opens at 8:30 a.m. The grass is burnt, the sky is grey and it is on its way to feels-like-38-degrees-Celsius, so Mindimooyenh is using Robarts as their cooling station. They are dressed like a white lady in navy blue slacks, a white blouse and sensible beige sandals. They have their fake U of T student ID so they can access floors one through three of the stacks and use the computer. Mindimooyenh doesn't expect to be in Robarts very long. They expect to be sent to the medical library, because it wouldn't be research if it wasn't a goddamn wild goose chase.

Mindimooyenh's current research topic is neuroplasticity. It has only been in the last part of the twentieth century that zhaganash have learned that brains can change over the course of an individual's life. Of course Mindimooyenh has always known that the brain is a relational organ, that it is constantly building and rebuilding networked pathways, constantly removing or reconnecting synaptic pathways. Brain as ecosystem. Repetitive thoughts and actions wiring and rewiring the brain.

You are what you do, as Akiwenzii says.

Mindimooyenh believes this is the function of ceremony. Ceremony strengthens the prefrontal cortex — the part of the brain responsible for emotional regulation and empathy. Ceremony is not just one big dumping ground of sharing circle. It is not a performance. It is not even necessarily designed to make you feel better.

It is exercise. The repetitive meditative nature. The long hours. Continually bringing wandering distracted minds back into the presence strengthens the prefrontal cortex, releases neurotransmitters like serotonin, dopamine and melatonin, killing anxiety, depression, addictions and insomnia.

Exercise that widens the network and tightens the connection. Exercise that produces and reproduces love.

Mindimooyenh is writing all of this down in tiny notebooks that open vertically and fit into the palm of their hand. They are using ballpoint pens they stole from hotel lobbies and banks.

MINDIMOOYENH

Mindimooyenh writes in the middle of their yellow notebook on the light blue lines:

"Ceremony is not about Creator."

Lucy is in the bush sleeping and dreaming and this is when Mindimooyenh comes back to read their research notebooks out loud as if Lucy weren't there. Mindimooyenh uses the first names of researchers whose papers they have sort of read parts of like they know them personally. Mixed in with the science, Mindimooyenh also has meticulous notes about the weather, the prices of the things they purchased that day and what they ate.

Lucy finds the research both interesting and irritating. Irritating because there is a quality to it that seems appropriative, like white-people mindfulness and yoga. Interesting because it seems like the key to everything. Irritating because it's never that easy, it couldn't possibly work that well and hardly anyone goes into ceremony with an open heart anymore anyway.

Mindimooyenh shows up for the four nights at dusk and reads their notes anyway. On days they don't go into the city or on the computer, it is just a list of things they ate.

LUCY

Lucy is having a dream about Ninaatig walking around downtown Toronto on their roots. In the dream, it is easier than one might think, because no one but kids and birds really pays attention to where trees are and no one believes kids or birds. Still, Ninaatig is stealthy, and moves quickly and then rests for a long while. Lucy would like it if Ninaatig could follow them. Ninaatig mostly hangs out in the Don Valley on the right side of Rosedale Valley Road where the Nishnaabeg and their friends have their tents. They also live in the sky and the earth and the present, so Ninaatig feels less lonely.

The city is not Ninaatig's favourite, but that's where the work is, and so that's where Ninaatig is, at least during the warm weather. They spend most of their nights on the right side of Rosedale Valley Road with Adik and sometimes Sabe, but lately, they have been heading down to the lake to Tommy Thompson Park. There is a kid there that needs them too. The kid just doesn't know it yet.

The kid has a red glow to them like when rock gets heated up in the sweat. They spend all their time thinking about birds but not in the usual way humans think about birds, more in the way birds think of themselves, Ninaatig notes. This kid is a bit too fearless, in that they are spending more and more nights in the park, lying amongst the shrubs and trees as if they were part of the landscape, sometimes lighting the tiniest of fires, almost theoretical. Ninaatig worries the most about Asin, they sure do. This kid gets barely enough REM sleep to function and is always down here talking with the birds all night, writing weird poems in an overpriced notebook.

Ninaatig doesn't get it. But they rub Asin's back beside the tiny fire anyway. Maybe Akiwenzii can straighten this little nutbar out, they think.

To be honest, if anyone is going to get Asin, it should be Ninaatig. It's just that you certainly do not know what you've lost until it's gone and Ninaatig still has the birds. They still visit hourly. They still come for tea and to catch up. They still build their homes in Ninaatig's branches. They still say goodbye before their long trips. They still tell Ninaatig all the stories, and gift the world with their young in Ninaatig's canopy. They still sing all the songs. This is so normal for Ninaatig that it is Ninaatig, and so they can't imagine a reality without it.

Unlike Asin. Asin lives with the hole and is driven to fill it.

Asin is interested in the behaviour of birds, but not in the way that behavioral ecologists are interested, not within the enclosure of Western science or evolution, so when Asin is birdwatching in Tommy Thompson Park, every single day of the year at dusk, they are watching something quite different than everyone else.

Asin is watching for bird ethics. They are watching for how birds interact and communicate with each other. They are watching for how bird communities understand consent, care, self-determination, sovereignty. They are watching for queerness.

When Asin is not at work at the community radio station, and not at Tommy Thompson Park, they are watching the birds at their feeder, which is located on their fire escape. They are reading about birds. They are taking online courses from the Cornell Lab of Ornithology. They are checking various birdwatching apps for the locations of rare species, and they are watching. They are always watching.

Asin is careful with the birding books, the websites and the apps and they treat the knowledge in them as suspect. The base for Asin is the things Akiwenzii has told them. The stories of the Bineshiinyag of when the earth was just being built. Bineshiinyag as carries and movers and spreaders and processes of knowledge through their relationship with seeds. This is the sole reason Asin watches, and they don't watch with their eyes and their brain, they watch with their heart and their muscles.

ASIN

There are lots of people interested in Asin for reasons that baffle Asin. They are always the last one to know. They also think it's just friends and nothing else, even though that's almost never the case. There is a string of disappointed hearts, some of them even broken, trailing Asin because their needs have not been met. Asin barely notices. Asin is often challenged by love and humans. It is only within Asin's capacity to practice those kinds of relations with birds. Particularly the boreal owl they have been watching for four winters now.

ASIN

Asin knows the word for owl is kookooko'oo. But they don't know the word for boreal owl. Akiwenzii is trying to remember but so far they can only remember gaakaabishiinh, which is a screech owl. Akiwenzii doesn't get why Asin is so obsessed with this damn owl, anyway. The old people didn't even like owls. They thought they were bad omens, a warning to start paying better attention.

Asin gets frustrated with Lucy's radio silence. It has been three days and they don't understand what Lucy could possibly be doing that means they cannot type three words into the phone and press send. Particularly when they know Asin's mental health depends upon it. It's hard for Asin to believe this is not deliberate. Lucy is smart. Asin has used their words repeatedly. It cannot be this difficult to learn how to love Asin. Asin has set the terms out fairly clearly.

Asin also knows the pattern. Late on the fourth day, Lucy's text will show up dripping with missing and loving and Asin won't buy it, not one little bit. Lucy will persist. Asin will break down and by day seven it's back to normal. Every time.

It isn't exactly a secret that Lucy takes off every month for four days to fast. As in, Lucy has never set out to hide it. They just didn't tell anyone the first time, or the second time. Then it became part of the routine. Part of how they gathered courage. Lucy has no idea how Mindimooyenh found out. They just showed up with their big purse full of lists one day. Lists and baggies.

Lucy's lodge is at the back of Akiwenzii's property and beside the dump. The saplings they used to build it are not exactly saplings. They are wire frames from the election signs when Sean Conway ran for the NDP. Lucy didn't feel right about killing saplings to make the lodge when there was a big stack of useless signs on the ground, so they fashioned the ribs out of their lodge with the wire. It worked fine. It felt good.

A book Asin does spend a considerable amount of time with in a less suspicious way is *Biological Exuberance: Animal Homosexuality and Natural Diversity* by Bruce Bagemihl, Ph.D. Asin is particularly drawn to the section on Canada geese. They read pages 483 and 484 over and over until it is paraphrased into their brain with a particular rhythm. Two Canada geese of the same sex sometimes pair-bond. Sometimes they even form triads, usually two females and a male. Sometimes, one of the females will mount another female. Some lesbian pairs raise a family. Then an example of two lesbians is relayed in which one partner built a nest and laid eggs while the other stood guard, and then the other partner built her own nest next to the first and also laid eggs. None of the eggs hatched, though, because they constantly rolled the eggs (which may or may not have been fertile) between the two nests and broke them all.

Asin sees only the purest form of love.

The passage then goes on to explain how snow geese are better lesbian parents than Canada geese, because they build only one nest and lay twice the eggs of the heterosexual couples.

Asin never finds it easy to read the words "mount" and "copulate."
Nor are they happy with the assumptions that Bruce makes about
Canada goose lesbians. Nor are they happy about the trauma porn
Bruce has created out of the tragedy this young lesbian couple faced.
Nor are they happy these are the two paragraphs in the book they
are drawn to. Nor are they happy that snow geese are always the
higher-end geese.

Asin eventually gets to page 485 and, after reading the part about
snow geese there, they reconsider their take on the snow goose, and
then rip the page out of the book, because anthropologists, even bird
anthropologists, generally get most things wrong and anthropology
is always more about your own bias than the thing you are studying.

Asin tries to remember this in Tommy Thompson Park.

There are things Lucy wants to add to their life and they think about these things one time a month during the fast in the bush beside the dump. They want to hunt. They do hunt deer, but they've never killed one. They want to hunt one, kill it, skin it, and tan the hide with the brain. There are some problems, though. No one on the reserve remembers how to tan hides with brains. This is not an overwhelming obstacle, though, because the Dene know how and they are experts. They can even do it in the city in front of tourists and protect those hides from every bad zhaganash thought that tries to penetrate them. The biggest problem is that Akiwenzii can't move around in the bush like they used to, so Lucy and Akiwenzii hunt from the truck and on short walks in a farmer's field — the one farmer that will give them permission. The real problem, though, is that Lucy is a bad shot. A real bad shot. They need more practice.

LUCY

Lucy thinks: Things unfold in good time.

Lucy thinks: Sometimes you have to make things happen.

Lucy thinks: There is a tension between unfolding and making.

Asin can only sleep for more than two hours at a time if there is a fire. Summer in the city presents a huge problem, because although Asin was able to find an apartment with a fireplace, they cannot find an outside location in the city where they can build a fire and so sleep deprivation is their current norm.

> *Open air burning includes bonfires, fire pits, sky lanterns and the use of various types of outdoor fireplaces (also known as a "Chiminea"). Although outdoor fireplaces can be purchased at retail outlets throughout the city, it does not mean open air burning is permitted for their use.*

> *Open air burning is not permitted within the City of Toronto and is enforceable under Ontario Fire Code Article 2.4.4.4.*

Asin has tried a candle.

Asin has tried YouTube videos of fire.

Asin has tried renting the campfire pits at Dufferin Grove Park.

Asin has tried lighting a fire in their backyard fire pit, but on day three the Fire Department showed up because the zhaganash neighbour lady called "out of concern."

Asin has tried lighting the fire in the fireplace and using the air conditioner at the same time to keep the temperature reasonable but the fire was too strong a force.

Asin has tried to make a campfire smell out of a concoction of essential oils but what they created was more like Pine-Sol.

The bottom line is, if Asin wants to sleep for more than two hours in a row, they need to get out of this city.

Which was exactly Akiwenzii's plan all along.

FOUR

PLASTICISM

MINDIMOOYENH

Mindimooyenh says: "Tarps are made out of polyethylene."

Mindimooyenh says (quoting Wikipedia): "As of 2017, over 100 million tonnes of polyethylene resins are produced annually, accounting for 34% of the total plastics market."

MINDIMOOYENH

Their heart sinks.

MINDIMOOYENH

Their heart sinks.

AKIWENZII

Akiwenzii says: "one tonne = one thousand kilograms."

AKIWENZII

Every morning Akiwenzii gets up at biidaaban. Biidaaban comes at a slightly different time every day so Akiwenzii gets up at a slightly different time every day. They walk down to the lake at the end of their property. They put tobacco. They pray. They sing four songs to the water, and then most mornings, tears leak, because with water there is affinity.

Every night since June 21, Akiwenzii drives to Kinomagewapkong at 11 p.m. to sleep on the rocks. It's the only place they can sleep for more than two hours in a row, so in the summer they sneak back here at night as much as possible. Their Elder status gives them the key and as long as they are gone by 4:45 a.m., before the first dog-walkers show up in the park, they can get in and out undetected. Plus it is cool there in the summer and there are no mosquitoes.

Akiwenzii parks the truck in the closed parking lot, goes through the chain-link fence, locking it behind them, and opens the door of the building Ontario Parks has built over the site. They slip off their moccasins, put down their pipe and drum and roll out onto the rock after they put some semaa down and speak to the rock.

They turn off all the power and the security cameras because they are allowed to if ceremony. Akiwenzii lies down with their head on one of the deep crevices. They wake up at 11:55 p.m., hardly enough sleep, but just enough time to carve.

AKIWENZII

The next night, Akiwenzii lies down with their head on one of the deep crevices. They wake up at 11:55 p.m., hardly enough sleep, but just enough time to carve.

AKIWENZII

The next night, Akiwenzii lies down with their head on one of the deep crevices. They wake up at 11:55 p.m., hardly enough sleep, but just enough time to carve.

AKIWENZII

The next night, Akiwenzii lies down with their head on one of the deep crevices. They wake up at 11:55 p.m., hardly enough sleep, but just enough time to carve.

The next night, Akiwenzii lies down with their head on one of the deep crevices. They wake up at 11:55 p.m., hardly enough sleep, but just enough time to carve.

The next night, Akiwenzii lies down with their head on one of the deep crevices. They wake up at 11:55 p.m., hardly enough sleep, but just enough time to carve.

Asin's hole is similar to Adik's. Similar but also different. Centuries ago, Adik had family. Herd. They had land, culture, endless song. They had language. They had all the essentials of living one's best life. Now all that is gone and Adik lives in the realm of a dangerous loneliness, where every connection is only a little bit right, and none is effortless. They are never really seen. There is nothing Ninaatig can do to alleviate this reality. Not a single thing. It is just something Adik lives alongside.

Adik's favourite place is Kinomagewapkong. There are adikwag carvings. There is the sound of Akiwenzii's gneiss hammer. There are the five-lined skinks. Ninaatig likes to visit Kinomagewapkong too, and in the summer, they go every night with Adik to help Akiwenzii sleep.

Adik walks over to Kinomagewapkong at night to check in on Akiwenzii. The water in McGinnis Lake tastes like water, for one thing, and Adik is a worrier. They are not sure what this old man is doing sleeping on the rock every night, and getting so little sleep at that. Adik circles Akiwenzii four times, licks their cheek and then heads back to the Don Valley. Worst-case scenario, Adik thinks, is that Akiwenzii dies here — and what a spectacular place to change existence.

Adik and Akiwenzii have been together forever. Adik remembers the day Akiwenzii was born in the bush on the reserve with an old kookum who served as both the midwife and the undertaker. They remember the songs for when Akiwenzii was in the birth canal. They remember the songs for when Akiwenzii came through the doorway. They remember the feast and the thanksgivings for this new life.

Adik didn't spend a lot of time with Akiwenzii until Akiwenzii was supposed to be in school. That's when Adik saw opportunity, and they regularly busted him out and took him into the bush to hang out with them and Sabe, and sometimes even Ninaatig. Akiwenzii was not difficult to lure out of school and into the bush. They did that all on their own anyway. Adik just made sure they were safe from all forms of kid-snatchers. They made sure the bush was like a hug. They made sure Akiwenzii was fed well.

In the spring, Adik, Akiwenzii and Sabe ate duck and turtle eggs. In the summer, they picked buckets full of berries, tended the garden and fished. In the fall, they were the busiest. They riced. They harvested the garden and cached it away for later. They hunted ducks and geese. They hunted deer and moose, dried meat and tanned hides. In the winter — well, in the winter, they told stories, sewed, drank buckets full of tea, fished through the ice and then told more stories. Then they repeated the pattern.

Adik and Sabe also taught Akiwenzii about old-time ceremony, and when they did this, they went north, deep into the bush, well out of reach of anyone. They built lodges, fasted, sweat, prayed and sang.

It was never perfect, but it was always good enough.

MINDIMOOYENH

Mindimooyenh has one app on their phone and it is Al Jazeera. Their notifications are turned on for Palestine. They dream of a Jayco trailer houseboat. They dream of driving their Jayco house trailer boat all the way to Palestine with the flotilla to resist the idea that this situation is complicated, that there are two sides, that there is no way to help.

MINDIMOOYENH

Mindimooyenh dreams of a houseboat. More of a floating dock than a boat, more of a trailer than a house, but a trailer houseboat with a brand-new Evinrude all the same.

MINDIMOOYENH

Mindimooyenh keeps their special things zippered into their front pocket:

fishing line and a needle

baggie full of assorted buttons

nail clippers

MINDIMOOYENH

Mindimooyenh says: "The Palestinian people are our cherished relatives."

MINDIMOOYENH

They say "cherished" as if it were a ritual.

AKIWENZII

After a week of carving, Akiwenzii makes "(C_2" appear on the rock face using their gneiss hammer. Akiwenzii misses Adik.

Akiwenzii lies down with their head on one of the deep crevices. They wake up at 11:55 p.m., hardly enough sleep, but just enough time to carve. After two weeks of carving, "$(C_2H$" is embedded onto the rock face. They use a gneiss hammer. Akiwenzii misses Sabe. They try to remember the last time they saw that old one.

AKIWENZII

Akiwenzii is wondering when someone is going to notice that they are carving on the rocks at Kinomagewapkong. They have been sneaking back almost every night all summer and while their modifications on the rock are tiny, they would have thought someone would have noticed something by now. Not that they are upset by this. They don't need to get charged for defacing a sacred site. They don't need to try and explain that one can't just look at or preserve a sacred site. That if the sacredness is to be maintained, Nishnaabeg have to continue the relationship. Fast. Pray. Sing. Carve. You cannot just ignore something and expect it to still be there for you when you need it.

FIVE

AMPLIFICATION

ADIK

Adik's favourite sound is ten thousand hooves hitting the ice. Imagine. You can't even.

Adik was sitting on the east side of Rosedale Valley Road during rush hour when a Mercedes loaded with zhaganash family was driving by at a snail's pace because of the traffic. Adik could tell that things were not good in the back seat by the lightning bolts coming out of that region of the car, and just as Mom accelerated, the five-year-old zhaganash rolled down their window and threw their aqua-blue Fjällräven Kånken mini-backpack out the window. It landed at Adik's feet.

The backpack was rectangular. Cheap on the straps. Could maybe get $40 on Kijiji for it.

Inside the Kånken was a nursery school painting on newsprint of who knows what in primary blue and primary red, folded into quarters. Ish. Five rocks and a piece of asphalt. A gull feather. An uneaten package of MadeGood granola balls — banana flavour. Adik ate those, unfolded the painting and hung it inside Sabe's plastic water bottle lodge and threw the rocks and asphalt into the bush.

ADIK

Adik did not know a lot about backpacks but they did know that this one carried a certain ethic and status with it, even though the straps were cheap.

ADIK

Adik loosened the straps all the way and tried it on, because why not.

They kept it on for the rest of the day, because why not.

They decided to keep it, because it was a gift, and one should keep gifts.

ADIK

After the fourth day of wearing the backpack, Adik moved their special things into it:

exhibition catalogue to Jeneen Frei Njootli's *I can't make you those mitts because there is a hole in my heart and my hands hurt*

tin of spruce gum balm for their hooves

voice recorder

ADIK

Adik records the sound of the bush as Ninaatig pushes their shopping cart towards them.

Adik's hooves are always sore. Always. It is because they are designed for moss, earth and snow and all there is now is concrete and asphalt. When Adik is at Akiwenzii's cabin, Akiwenzii lets Adik use Dr-Ho's Circulation Promoter and wow that thing is worth its weight in gold. The rest of the time, Adik rubs spruce gum balm into the cracks and hopes for the best.

Akiwenzii always says, "Take it! You need it more than me!"

But Adik never does. It won't fit into their backpack for one thing and where would they get thirty-eight AAA batteries anyway. Plus it's a nice part of visiting Akiwenzii, something to look forward to doing. Looking forward to things is important.

Adik does record the sound of the foot massages and the sounds of relief Akiwenzii makes when they are using said massager.

ADIK

Adik stops into Artspace in Nogojiwanong on their way back from Kinomagewapkong to see Jeneen Frei Njootli's exhibition. Adik had been there for the installation because how could they miss that really, but the best part was the opening, because Frei Njootli had invited the Porcupine caribou herd to attend with her. And wow wow wow. Here Adik was, in their own territory, dancing to Frei Njootli's sounds with the only living relatives they had ever known, while all the humans stood around acting impressed and dumbfounded or whatever they did when they attended arts shows not really made for them at all. The installation is called *I can't make you those mitts because there is a hole in my heart and my hands hurt.* They sure made mitts that night, though.

Adik shelled out the $20 to get the catalogue with essays by Olivia Whetung in it that Adik promised themselves they would read later, mostly so they'd have a physical reminder of the dancing. They put the catalogue carefully in their Kånken backpack for later. Adik wishes Jeneen could see them. They wish Jeneen could see them and would take them home to the Gwich'in, who would know just what to do.

Adik took the adikwag up to Kinomagewapkong after the opening was over. They wanted to show them their bush, and the carvings of the caribou on the rock. Adik wanted to repay them for the purity of the early evening, and this was the only way they thought to do it.

Akiwenzii was there sleeping.

ADIK

The main thing Adik wants to do with the adikwag at Kinomagewapkong is to record the sound of their hooves on the rock. They set up the recorder and give Akiwenzii a kick so that they roll over, stop snoring and ruining the recording. Then the adikwag just walk in a sunwise direction around the rock, and Adik records.

It is like adding a drummer to the band.

Adik likes to keep on the move, even though that is no longer easy in Michi Saagiig Nishnaabeg territory. They take the ferry over to the island with the tourists in the summer. They wander up to the Rouge Valley to visit the moist, and sometimes they stroll out into Tommy Thompson Park with Ninaatig. Ninaatig has a project by the name of Asin in the park, and they like to check on the kid. They have a real thing for birds.

Every ziigwan, Adik spends time with Lucy and Sabe tapping trees at Akiwenzii's. This past year was the fourth season in a row, and for the most part it was just the three of them. Lucy with the drill and then the ATV, collecting the buckets of sap. Sabe on fire. Adik and Lucy taking turns watching the boil. Adik liked the rhythm of it, the busy. They liked being with Sabe and Lucy for long hours with a common goal. They liked the warmth of the sugar shack and the sweet smell of Ninaatigoog.

It is the only time of the year when Adik's hooves stop hurting.

At least one of the nights when Adik, Lucy and Sabe are boiling during the day, Adik walks up to the gorge on the Crowe River. The gorge is magnificent, and it is where some very skilled and knowledgeable water creatures live. Adik isn't there to see them, though. Adik is there to record the sound of water carving out rock. Adik is there to record the language of the past talking to the present. Adik is there to record the sound of hope.

Adik bought the Sony UX Series Digital Voice Recorder in Black from Best Buy. The recorder is rechargeable, and so Adik makes sure they plug it in at Akiwenzii's house, and that keeps their visits to Akiwenzii regular. The recorder records for 159 hours.

Adik's plan is to record the gorge for twelve hours. They move down to the flat rock closest to the river, set up the recorder, press record and then fall asleep.

ADIK

Adik heads up to Kinomagewapkong at dusk. They tie a string to the voice recorder, press play and lower it between the sides of the big crevice. Adik smiles. Tonight when Akiwenzii lies down and puts their ear to the rock, things will be as right as they can be — just like before the zhaganash built the building and choked off the creek. Akiwenzii will hear the water. Akiwenzii will hear the world.

At dusk, after a day in the city, Sabe rides their bike to Tommy Thompson Park. They are not watching the birds, though. They watch this oddball kid who is obsessed with birds — a boreal owl in the winter, and in the summer, any one of the fifty nesting species in the park. The kid has a deep red glow about them, like an ancestor stone when they are about to come out of the fire and into the lodge. Asin is an odd duck to be sure. They have all the usual equipment — phone, bird books, notebooks, but they don't do any of the same things the other birders do, and this is why Sabe is drawn to them. They sort of just sit and feel. Sometimes, late at night, they build the tiniest of fires and fall asleep. This is when Sabe shows up to rub Asin's back.

AKIWENZII

The next night, Akiwenzii lies down with their head on one of the deep crevices. They wake up at 11:55 p.m., hardly enough sleep, but just enough time to carve. After four weeks, "$(C_2H_4$" is embedded onto the rock face. Akiwenzii misses Ninaatig. They try to think of the last time they saw that old one.

That final night, they wake up at 11:55 p.m., hardly enough sleep, but just enough time to finish carving "$(C_2H_4)n$" into the rock face using their gneiss hammer.

Sabe and Adik arrive to witness.

Sabe brings Akiwenzii's special things from the glove compartment of their truck:

claw of an eagle wrapped in red cloth

flint and steel

hunting knife

Sometimes Lucy and Akiwenzii set up a practice target outside the sugar shack. One time it was an old door. Akiwenzii drew a target on the door with a Sharpie and Lucy attempted to shoot at it. Lucy needs more practice than Akiwenzii can provide, mainly because the wasting of ammunition is driving Akiwenzii bonkers. Lucy can unload thirty shots and hit the circle once or twice. In Akiwenzii's day, that would be thirty deer, not one tiny paint chip in an old door. They think about going to a gun range. Akiwenzii thinks that's dangerous and ridiculous and after the Possession and Acquisition Licence course, they highly doubt Sabe will accompany them. So, it's back to the door.

Akiwenzii thinks screens have ruined Lucy's eyes and that this entire generation is hopeless. They put that in their do-not-say bin. Not that Lucy could hear anyway, because they are wearing hearing protection so the sound doesn't cause their body to involuntarily jump in fear.

Akiwenzii does not know how one can possibly hunt if one can't hear the animal coming. They put that in their do-not-say bin too.

LUCY

To be honest, Lucy isn't looking forward to the processing of the deer, to facing the death they caused. The gutting and quartering is going to be real. Too real. Blood. Guts. Smell. Plus hide-tanning requires a very old kind of patience and work ethic Lucy isn't sure they possess. It is a very concentrated kinetics where one doesn't move across the land, but one still travels a great distance, they presume.

LUCY

Lucy is just waking up on the fourth day when Asin arrives with the blanket. They have only a tiny bit more of stitching on the border to do and then the thing is done. Asin had enough sense to bring food and water, and when they see the fire, they are overtaken with exhaustion. Lucy does the stitching. Asin falls asleep by the fire. The blanket is beautiful, all done in purples, reds and blues. The stars made out of tarp are Lucy's favourite part.

Several hours pass and Lucy completes the border of the blanket while Asin sleeps. After they finish the final stitch, the final knot and the final cut of thread with the scissors, Lucy puts the blanket down and looks up. There, not thirty feet away, is Waawaashkeshi, just standing and looking at Lucy.

Lucy looks back.

Waawaashkeshi lies down, still looking.

Lucy raises their 386 and fires, the bullet whistling through the air and hitting nothing.

Waawaashkeshi doesn't move, still looking.

Lucy fires again. The hemorrhaging begins.

Asin wakes up.

SIX

RECONFIGURATION

MINDIMOOYENH

Mindimooyenh is sitting on the cement wall at the edge of the canal watching teenagers jump off the old railroad bridge into the water. It looks dangerous. It is dangerous. But a sort of wholesome danger for teenagers these days, they think. They have to watch for cabin cruisers going through the lock and kayakers and canoeists.

Canoeists means white people in canoes. This is different than canoers, at least for Mindimooyenh, because they can remember when canoeing wasn't a thing, it was simply a means to an end. If you got there in an efficient way, you were fine. Over the course of your life you became good at it or you became dead at it. There were no personal floatation devices, or expensive paddles or whistles or Tilley hats. There were no badges or levels. It wasn't an exercise in choreography.

Today, the canoeists are moving through the canal in choreography, stopping, twirling, manoeuvring sideways with precision. Going nowhere fast, Mindimooyenh thinks.

Mindimooyenh is at the canal waiting for the sun to set. On nights like this, in the peak of summer, it takes forever. Within an hour of losing light, the canal becomes quiet and Mindimooyenh can sneak down to the rowing dock and fall asleep. They can only sleep for more than two hours on the water. The Jayco trailer houseboat will really solve a lot of problems.

SABE

Sabe needs to find Ninaatig, but Ninaatig isn't in their usual place in Mark S. Burnham Park in Nogojiwanong. It's proving more difficult than normal. It's easier to track humans and animals. Way easier. Ninaatig leaves very little behind, very little to go on.

Sabe is ready to admit they are struggling, maybe ... and need help. At least in the dead of night they are ready to make that admission. Most times by morning the rhythm of daylight lulls them into some other kind of coping.

What Sabe needs is Ninaatig to hold them while they sleep. It is the only way they can sleep more than two hours in a row. Ninaatig holds and sucks the hurt, the pain, the broken right out of them. They've been doing it for centuries.

Sabe believes that they should be able to self-soothe and self-heal themselves, so they imagine holding themselves all through the night. This doesn't bring on sleep. It brings on a kind of calm that is better than no calm, but it doesn't fix the dull ache in their lower back or the desperation in their throat.

Sabe goes outside and peeks under the tarp with the 250-ml water bottles. After tomorrow morning's run, they will have enough to build another shelter. At first, Sabe planned to sew the noses of six bottles together into a star formation like the first one, and then sew all the stars together into a domed lodge for their buds on the east side of Rosedale Valley Road. A tarp over that would make a fine lodge. Now, they are reconsidering. The star formation looks pretty, for sure, but they could make many more structures by simply making curved poles out of the water bottles, more like the saplings you'd use to make a sweat. The star design seems more meaningful, on account of the stars — though six-pointed stars don't carry a lot of weight in Nishnaabeg cosmology and Sabe wonders if the water bottles in this dense a formation will be hot and if they will off-gas as they decompose and they know it is always okay to sacrifice meaning for functionality, except of course when meaning brings forth Nishnaabeg joy.

Sabe wonders what they have gotten themselves into. Their building skills are fine for the bush, but adapting to new materials on the fly without research suddenly feels stupid, like they could be doing something more useful with their time.

Mindimooyenh is one of my parents and when they are not nervous, they say only five to ten words per day, but when they are nervous, they just talk and talk and talk and it doesn't matter if you listen or pay attention or respond or talk to them back. I didn't realize the extent of this until I was in the lake. Right now they are talking about sleeping in cars because they are scared of bears and it wouldn't be the first time and it won't be the last time. They are talking about babysitting three grandbabies and feeding and changing them and getting it all organized in an assembly line so no one is crying. They are talking about Numbnuts and at first I forget who he is, but as they go on I remember and he better hope they never run into him again.

They are talking about cooking roasts and turkeys for the feast in eight different slow cookers in the basement apartment where they stay and they hope they don't blow a fuse because then how will they cook the turkeys and the roasts for the shelter? They are talking about fans from the dollar store. They are talking about saving $100 worth of petunias from their neighbour's garden.

When I was a kid, my younger sister pored over the Sears catalogue every night for three months, picking out the exactly right plastic white doll Santa Claus was going to bring them. Their final choice was one with a soother, which they called a "dody plug," a mop of blonde psycho hair and a soft cloth body for hugging. By March, the white plastic head had been loved right off, and Mindimooyenh was having none of it. The doll was expensive, even though Santa and their elves had made it in their workshop at the North Pole and it had been delivered by deer-sled. The doll was getting sent back to Mattel in the original box and they were going to fix it for Santa and send the doll back to us. Fixed. This posed a challenge, because the original box had been more fun to play with than the original doll, and in its morphing from box to time machine to Easy-Bake Oven to mailbox to hat, it had fallen apart. No worries. The grocery store has free boxes. Don't be so stupid. But there are no lids. Don't be so stupid. We will just wallpaper her in there with the extra wallpaper from when we made the front room fancy for the bridge club ladies by pasting over our grubbiness. And so this is how I found my seven-year-old self facing the mean post office lady with a headless dead doll in a wallpapered no-lid box coffin. She examined the box. She poked the box. She queried. And then she threw the box across the post office until it hit the wall and the doll's head flew out through the wallpaper. "There," she said, "you can't send that."

I took the box home, unsure if Mindimooyenh would believe my story of the projectile package. They did. And they took that box and wallpapered it and wallpapered it and wallpapered it, and then they packed everyone into the red plastic toboggan and we stormed back to the post office and Mindimooyenh demanded to see Canada Post's policy on wallpaper which the mean lady could not produce, and off the box went to the North Pole, never to be seen again.

On our way out, the mean post office lady yelled that Mindimooyenh could no longer just Scotch tape the correct amount of change to their letters and mail them, that they had to buy stamps like everyone else.

As if Mindimooyenh will ever buy stamps like everyone else.

MASHKAWAJI

I go over and over the last time I saw Sabe. I was in the city in a hotel and Sabe was with me.

Sabe tells me from the bed to just call down to the lobby and find out when the first shuttle bus goes to the airport, but I insist on taking the elevator down to the front desk and reading the sign so I won't have to talk to anyone because what could possibly go wrong. I was thinking I could "rehydrate" at the fancy lemon water station beside the stuffed dead black bear on my way back up to the room instead of drinking the exact same sink water out of the bathroom, and this would count as self-care for the day.

I'm reading the sign and letting the 4:45 a.m. departure time sink in, sipping the lemon water in the shitty plastic cup, when he approaches me with all the confidence the trifecta of obliviousness and delusion and patriarchy can provide.

We talk about things, but not really, because I can't remember who he is.

He tells me he's the director general of Indian Affairs and sometimes I have a poker face and sometimes I just have a face.

He is so clean and shiny. I'm in flannel plaid pyjama pants with a not-matching plaid flannel shirt because who gives a fuck. He has a bureaucratic overcoat and adult shoes that require regular neoliberal maintenance. I'm in bare feet. He looks like he's lived in Ottawa for too long. I look like I've lived in Peterborough for too long.

I remind myself to try not to give up completely, at least not all the time.

He says sentences like "we are making good progress" and he means it.

I laugh at the "we" and the "progress" and I mean it too.

I think of flying over Chi'Nibish and the feeling I get when I look down. The flat blue going off in all directions hiding the poison that is not its own in the sediments that cradle its very being.

Then I remember the speech his dad gave at his wedding in Oshawa, after he married a white girl in Niagara Falls. I remember his dad called him "bucko" when he was little. I remember him rubbing my lower back in his parents' basement in 1994 in Prince George and the moment I decided not to turn it into something. I remember him telling me to be careful because the cab driver that picked him up from my apartment thought I was hot and had a knife under the passenger seat.

I remember when his baby died.

I remember last Christmas, when I paid $5 and filed a Freedom of Information request to see how much data CSIS and Indian Affairs had on me, and how when the package came it was small, because there was so much they had to burn it onto a CD-ROM. I put a red ribbon through the hole in the CD-ROM and hung it on the tree beside the Tears for Fears CD.

Here we are on the cold tile floor of the lobby. Just the three of us. Him, me, the barbed wire.

Him in charge of the line between getting fucked and getting fucked over. Me in charge of yelling down an empty hall.

He thinks this is a nice, chance encounter, but that's not what I'm thinking. He thinks we are on the same side, reconciliation and all that.

I'm thinking of the lake again. And how government scientists use a contraption to collect sediments from the bottom of a lake called an Ekman grab. It is a metal box on a string, with claws on the end. You trip it and the claws close, taking a sample of the bottom. The scientists put the samples in Ziploc bags and use Sharpies to write coordinates on the front. The scientists send them to the lab. The results always come back the same: they were right and there is nothing to be done because because.

There is an important difference between testing and caring.

It's in these moments that I know I'm still so, so hurt.

You can fall into toxic sediments at the bottom of your heart and not come out for months.

I go back to my room with the nausea of betrayal in my gut and together we dwell on why I misjudged him or how I misjudged him. Sabe and I pore over the archives for missed red flags, evidence that was overlooked, missed interventions. On why this particular knife hurts. On how it is that in 1978, he was an Asian kid getting beat up and I was an NDN kid getting beat up and now all there is is just this.

Sabe says, "Don't go to the lobby in your bare feet," and we both laugh. Sabe makes a campfire about it and they order Domino's pizza, even though we could have done better, and we watch episode after episode of white people renovating their houses on my laptop.

I think about how the lake is more beautiful holding your hurt, and how I'll drink the lake any day, because light is better than no light.

I think about how the last thing we did in that lobby was hug goodbye, but it wasn't like a chair massage, it was like an email you don't return, it was like releasing the claws of the Ekman that grab, like letting the collected sediments fall back into the lake, because we already know the results.

MASHKAWAJI

There is nothing Ninaatig hates more than coming to visit me. Frozen is a panic attack for them. They hate being on water and on ice and they've only made the trip once so far and I love them to pieces for trying. By the time they get here with the damn shopping cart, they are so upset all they can do is two strokes of a back rub and then they have to get off the water and back onto dry land.

Adik comes to visit one time too in the spring, but they are quiet and mostly don't talk. I notice Adik has a new fancy backpack, though. It was nice to be close to them. They recorded the sound of the ice cracking and melting and then they packed up their backpack and wandered off.

LUCY

Sabe comes running when they hear the sound.

"It never rains, it pours," Sabe says, looking at the deer, Lucy and Asin. Sabe gets out their knife and tells Lucy and Asin to pay attention.

While Lucy, Asin and Adik watch Sabe fix Waawaashkeshi, Mindimooyenh stomps by and takes the finished blanket from Asin.

"Miigwech, not as bad as I was thinking. Nice tarp work," they say as they turn and stomp away.

LUCY

As Sabe makes the first cut, Waawaashkeshi whispers to Lucy, "Your real name is Biidaaban."

MINDIMOOYENH

Mindimooyenh says: "Wiindaawaso a'aw Akiwenzii."

Akiwenzii whispers to Lucy:

Gidizhinikaaz Biidaaban.

Gidizhinikaaz Biidaaban.

Gidizhinikaaz Biidaaban.

Gidizhinikaaz Biidaaban.

When Akiwenzii finishes the carving they are dead tired. They lie down in their usual place, on their side, using their arm as a pillow and pulling their knees to their chest. Ninaatig gently rubs their back. Adik walks around the rock, over and over. Sabe returns from Lucky's hunt, breaks the fire ban and lights a fire outside the building on the walkway.

They take their last breath.

Lucy starts removing the hair.

Asin sings all of the bird songs, starting with the song of the boreal owl.

SEVEN

LIFT

SABE

Sabe heads down to the road allowance where Mindimooyenh has parked their "boat." The Jayco trailer still has the wheels on and is sitting beside the water with no plan of how to get it onto the actual floating platform.

Sabe shakes their head and goes inside the trailer. It's way nice in there. Yes it is. The curtains and upholstery are fresh from the 1970s in various shades of green and with shapes that Sabe only knows as rectangles with U-shapes in various sizes all over them. There is fake-wood panelling. There are two tables that magically convert into double beds to augment the two double beds on each of the wings. Sabe chooses one of the wings to lie down on, scanning the fridge, the sink and the propane stove. Their idea was to give Mindimooyenh the lodge made out of plastic water bottles for the houseboat. But now, that seems cheap.

After a short nap, Sabe walks outside. Lifts the Jayco up over their head and gently lowers it onto the floating platform. They attach it as best they can with spruce roots and luck and mount the Evinrude to the back of the platform.

MINDIMOOYENH

Mindimooyenh arrives minutes later. "I guess that old one is paying better attention than I thought," they say to themselves.

MINDIMOOYENH

Mindimooyenh has a few more modifications to make before they are ready, the most important of which are attaching the feathers to the wings of the trailer and attaching the head. The code has to be exactly right for Binesiyag to recognize the structure as a scaffolding to inhabit — and while Mindimooyenh cares more about caring for others than protocol, this is one time where if they don't get the markings right, it's a pass/fail situation.

MINDIMOOYENH

Mindimooyenh steps off the land onto their houseboat. They undo the rope at the front and then the rope by the motor, and take one last look for Adik. It's not like them to be late. It's not like them to just ghost Mindimooyenh.

MINDIMOOYENH

Mindimooyenh turns the motor on, pleased they got the button kind with the steering wheel instead of the lawnmower kind that you have to pull and pull and pray to get started. They wonder if those assholes are going to show up at all, or if they should just leave without them, which seems to defeat the whole purpose.

The edge of the sun touches the horizon.

Mindimooyenh sees Sabe and the plastic water bottle sculpture out of the corner of their eye.

"What is that damn thing?"

"It might be useful."

"It is not useful and it is not coming."

"I'll just tie a rope to it and we'll pull it from behind. It floats. You never can tell when you might need a pre-fabricated plastic water bottle lodge on a trip like this."

MINDIMOOYENH

Mindimooyenh smiles.

AKIWENZII

Adik and Ninaatig step on board with Akiwenzii wrapped in the Starblanket Lucy and Asin stitched.

MINDIMOOYENH

Mindimooyenh thinks: It looks like they sewed that thing with their elbows, and the colour choice is a dog's breakfast.

They put that in their do-not-say bin.

SABE

Sabe smiles.

MINDIMOOYENH

Mindimooyenh switches the Chi-Jiimaan into gear and angles it out into the canal and they head towards the lake. After the tourists and the locks are gone, they glide through the mouth of everything, and Mindimooyenh and their floating beacons do not turn right towards the city with all the other boats. Instead, they continue straight south, towards the zone where the two shades of blue meet.

Sabe protests because the southern doorway is by all accounts the wrong way, but Mindimooyenh is steadfast.

"We have one more errand to do before the doorway. We need to pick up Mashkawaji. They are getting too cold."

The geese fly overhead singing songs of encouragement in the sheer grace of a carefully angled formation designed to take them elsewhere.

EIGHT

MASHKAWAJI'S THEORY OF ICE

the failure of melting

the frozen sighed
and gave up

the lake wrote
their letter of resignation

with the useful
uselessness
of despair

july 15
30 cubic metres
five storeys

your finger is
tracing nothing on my arm
as if we are the only ones here

i bring you coffee
a blanket
moonlight

i bring you stitches
a feather
three books

the caribou
sit
measuring emptiness

the fish
study
the methodology of giving up

the molecules
calculate
the accumulated effects of hate

you break
down
to a less ordered state

the ice
breathes
and gives in

the lake
runs
out of options

july 15
30 cubic metres
five storeys

just like
the Gwich'in
always said

there are all kinds
of ways
to fail.

head of the lake

in a basement full of plastic flowers
perogies and
cabbage rolls

at the head of the lake
thinking under accusation

at the mouth of the catastrophic river
disappearing our kids

at the foot of the nest
beside trailer hitches, coffee, spoons

we made a circle
and it helped

the smoke did the things
we couldn't

singing
broke open hearts

i hold your hand
without touching it.

we're in the thinking part of the lake
faith under accusation

at the mouth of the river
and the spectre of free

at the foot of Animikig
beside bones of stone and red silver

in a basement full of increasing entropy
moose ribs, wild rice.

in realization
we don't exist without each other

she says: there's nothing about you
i'm not willing to know.

death by water

boil your water
for twenty years
to remove
two parts road salt
one cup exhaust
two tablespoons of arsenic

biiwaanag
flint
tool
weapon
river

put the sign
in the forest so the
eagles see
put the sign
in the benthos
so the fish have
something to read

biiwaanag
flint
Black
Red
ignition

i'm sitting facing the wind
drinking in blue
her body around mine
lips tasting air

i love her anyway
i love her more. because.

biiwaanag
flint
spark
light
fire

weather

broken weather
irrevocable rain
injured creeks
and flood

basements ruined
internets caught on fire
burning from nothing to nothing
in green toxic blue flame

we sat on the log
again

in the absence of light
we picked ten dollar bills
our of each other's marrow

in the absence of rupture
we took turns
falling up into dreams

diving deeper and deeper
in the deficit of oxygen
through
insult and callout
through
ego and ego
swimming
drowning
sinking

i reach out
for my pawful of dirt
and instead
you hold my hand.

surface tension

there are beating wings
there are
simple
stolen
moments

the road only goes one way
and you can't get lost

the trees drive by
and we carry the river

i ask you four questions
you give me four answers:

the ininiwish that lived here
the book that saved your life

the akiwenzii that assigned you
the oil rig that only sang marx

we keep the critic in the back seat
i keep the answers in the hollow part of me

the river only goes one way
and you can't get lost

there are simple stolen moments
these are simple stolen moments

we love

when we are able

and there are beating wings reminding me
if you fly forever you can have two summers.

the wake

hello my friend
i've come
to see you again

everything we tried
to grow
this year has died

you're tripped inside my head
numb calm, dulled light
cold red

acorns and fallen stars
a child
that wasn't ours

ashes in my eyes
crushed fires
and shattered skies

wearing just the lake
diminished
in the wake

inside a commune of night
there's no way
to make this right

injured and certified
i wish i'd held you
when you died

you're tripped inside my head
numb calm, dulled light
cold red

everything we
tried to grow
this year has died.

cohesion

she fell into the lake
with a bag of tools

she patched the canoe with her shirt
and drove her kids across the river

she put ʔorı out
in the middle of lake

we soaked the hide
in ziibiins overnight

he carried his kid
even when they got lost

her water broke
and the door opened

they found her body
wrapped in a duvet

weighed down
with rocks

giigoonh picked her precious
out of their gills

held her forever
in their otoliths

aandeg watched

his last
breath

took his sound
embedded it in our heat

read his notes
and beaded them onto our hearts
promised his mama
we'd make it matter

we are all hunters
and we all knew

when white
strangles the trigger

we die twice.

viscosity

calling out
calling in
you're not fooling me

tethered to the kinship
of disassociated
zeros and ones

shining your crown
of neoliberal
likes

yelling the loudest
in the
empty room

gathering
followers
like berries

feeding
fish
to insecurity

sliding
into
reckless moment
after reckless moment

we witness:

too many holes in your hide
the broken skin of a canoe
the tightening of a mind
tracks, leading nowhere.

at the
beach
we build a fire

sit in our
own
silence

peel off
blue
light

lie back
on
frozen
waves

breathe
in
sharp air

warm
into
each other

careful moment
after careful moment.

break up

i step over
the watery edges

he pulls the canoe
across the ice

she paddles to the edge to collect candles
for her old ones to melt and then drink

you shoot ducks
while it's still easy.

they gather at the edge
thinking

they gather in the sky
rethinking

they swim towards light
thinking otherwise

sun hits you from above
you melt from inside out

faint ice as membrane
spreads sound across skin

aabawe the first warmth of spring
aabawe a loosening of the mind
aabawe to forgive

gathering into gatherings

they are watching in the front row
of the empty theatre
smiling through tears, remembering
going over and over in their minds

    they are this beautiful tendency to stick together.

a single nuclei of desert dust
falling 3.5 feet per second
falling 3.5 feet per second, but together
enfolding, one crystal at a time

    they are this beautiful tendency to stick together.

forming a nation of stunning difference
propagating arms of crystal
offering the full spectrum of possibility
reflecting the full spectrum of light

    they are this beautiful tendency to stick together.

zoogipo
    it is snowing
zoogipo
    aanakwad is giving birth
zoogipo
    a choir is falling from the sky
zoogipo
    building their bodies from time, temperature, circumstance

    they are this beautiful tendency to stick together.

there are six points
holding 10 quintillion molecules of water
mobilizing joy
amassing on aki

we are this beautiful tendency to stick together.

gashkadin :: freeze up

we gather
in the winter lodge
formed from earth
and ice

we slow
pray
sing
dream

earth below
world above
wait things out
but together.

my upper parts
are exiled to the bottom
my lower parts
deported to the surface

there is euphotic rising
and falling
orbits of dispossession,
reattachment

achieving
maximum density:
39 degrees fahrenheit,

lake as one mind.

i relax
at the surface
spread apart
cooler holding warmer

regular
repeated
ordered
locked

nurtured from the bottom up
leaving just enough
space
for this
incubated
life.

NINE

FORMATION

MANDAMINAAKOOG

Mandaminaakoog isn't in the best of shape. They aren't the best mathematician, or reader of the weather, and they aren't the best at details. They are, however, one of the most important individuals in formation, and while other societies might minimize the kind of work Mandaminaakoog does naturally, this one does not.

In the mornings, when navigation meets to refine the day's route and finalize logistics, Mandaminaakoog is quietly present. They watch the decision-making, the personalities, the egos. They take measure of who is able to see outside of themselves and make decisions easily and who struggles. They inventory mental and physical strain, and how the group manages, or doesn't manage. They answer questions when they are asked. They offer opinions when they are considered. They intervene only when the well-being of the formation is at risk, allowing the flock to fail and learn and recover and self-determine. They are wise, and their wisdom is of the kind that lived experience generates. A confidence that no matter what happens over the course of the day, they can handle it. They will always be okay. And of course when that isn't true, because it isn't true in life of any sort, there is an unwavering belief that they will handle it anyway.

They see the formation *as formation*. As a singular organism propelling itself to someplace else whose magnificence is bigger than the sum of its parts. Mandaminaakoog's responsibility is to observe the function of the system as a whole, to take note of inconsistencies and weaknesses. To watch how the system generates and uses energy, copes with and minimizes drag and friction and responds to the constantly changing variables of wind, temperature, moisture and light.

Sure the formation is made up of individuals and individuals are formations in and of themselves. But that is the trick. To not get caught up in one's own body, one's own experience, one's own cycling head. Synergy matters, because it represents the incomprehensible. The other forces and nations working with you even if you're unaware.

The wonder.

Mandaminaakoog has status, but status is never something that matters. What matters is commitment, desire, skill — and how those feed back on each other to create what appears from the outside to be an effortless elegance. What matters is showing up.

There will always be times in the journey where the unspoken and the interstitial spiral farther and farther down.

Times when the formation relies upon those good-natured ones that are never fooled by misfortunes, deterred by missteps or over-whelmed by the constant influx of changing variables. The ones that can change the feel of something instantaneously with a quick laugh. The ones who are almost always certain, and who remain calm even when they are uncertain. Confidence swimming in humility.

Humility, not as pity or a pathos. But as a lived realization that all of us, any of us, are just part of something more complex than we realize. That it is always less about the me.

What also matters is the nature of the individual, and this is dir-ectly correlated to skill level. Difficult individuals are tolerated if they have exceptional mastery of flight, but just as important as mastery is the ability to hold the group together; that makes the entire thing enjoyable. Most appreciated are the ones that can shift energy with a quick laugh or a diffuse response, those that pay attention to how bodies are feeling and then act accordingly. These individuals are just as crucial as those that can navigate, those that understand formation, logistics and engineering. The psychological management of individuals in formation, and of the formation itself, impacts all the other parameters of flight and migration in ways that few can predict.

Same with the network. Connecting the seat of each individual's character to the sequence is a constant job. Mandaminaakoog smudges everyone off at dawn and the flow will be strong, continually folding in. But by mid-morning three-quarters of the flock drops out of frequency without an inkling of notice, and they have virtually no skills to reconnect. This makes everyone's job more difficult. It's like flying in radio silence, out of range of support. Open channels inevitably fill with anxiety, and broken connections make the journey more of a cascading crisis than anything else. It is one thing after another, the group barely able to recover from the last crisis before the next one is upon them.

Mandaminaakoog needs to work with each individual on their own to teach them how to focus in and block out distraction, static and noise. They do this in the down times when the group isn't travelling, but it is a long road. It is a skill that requires enormous amounts of quiet practice, because the brain is literally rewriting and regrowing the synaptic pathways to make the focus happen — which is an elegant feat in and of itself. It makes it hard, though, for practitioners to believe, because it never seems like one is getting better at it. One always feels like a failure. Mandaminaakoog is also teaching how to sit with perpetual failing, or at least the perception that one is in perpetual failure.

Status is another imposition on an already difficult situation. In order to get border clearance, the state requires each migrating bird to have a certificate of status. The rules have changed over the years, and have become less stringent, but they have nothing to do with geese. They have nothing to do with anything other than the state's desire to regulate migrants out of existence, because controlling resident populations is much easier to manage if everyone just lives in the park all year around.

To obtain your migrant card, initially you need two parents that are migrants. In concert with the dispossession of airspace, breeding grounds, nesting grounds and places to live and be, and along with avian diseases and the near-destruction of the geese's world, this has proved to be devastating to the migrants. They also wholeheartedly reject carding and take whoever is best suited for the migration, doctoring cards and documents as needed.

This worked for a number of decades. It worked until the migrant-card rules relaxed, after the geese became so desiccated they were no longer perceived as a threat. There was a downside, though. The decades of cycling seeped into our guts. Resident populations had a different set of needs than the migrants. Words got mixed up.

"Weweni," those old ones whispered and no one heard.

"Weweni."

They meant, Be careful. Be very careful with your words. Your thoughts. Your actions. Think it through.

Then think it through again.

Think it ahead through time.

Think it backwards through time.

Find seven alternate ways to fix the problem.

Make sure it is a problem.

Make sure it needs to be fixed.

Think about the network as the first line of defence.

Think think think before you speak, type, post. Each syllable is a log you put on a fire. The fire can uplift or destroy.

Weweni.

Weweni.

Protect individual hearts from hurt, because the processing of hurt is necessary and it takes energy from the group. The supports needed to process trauma and to regenerate are costly.

Remember that words carry the ability to impact the chemistry of brains and the beating of hearts.

Calls should be whispers. The only one you can hold accountable is yourself. That really is your only job.

ASIN

Asin is waiting for the first ones to arrive.

There are signs in the ice if you can read ice code. Asin cannot.

There are signs in the position of the sun, and the time of dawn and dusk, if you can read sun code. Asin cannot.

There are signs in the positioning of stars, if you can read star code. Asin cannot.

There are signs because there are ones that come just before, and this Asin has a chance at reading, but not this year. Not this time.

Instead, Asin relies on eBird and when the first watchers report sightings on the south side of Lake Ontario.

Asin has spent the winter with residents in Tommy Thompson Park. They sit, like the meaning of their name, and watch. The geese certainly know Asin is there and they are somewhat interested in this one, this one with a notebook but no camera. This one that spends hours just watching.

SHKAABEWIS

Shkaabewis's position is on the left side, facing south, second from the back. It's considered one of the easier spots — those holding this position draft off of the ones in front and don't have to navigate. There is a monotony, though, in simply following the one ahead, beating wing after beating wing. That presents its own challenge, like being stuck on the vinyl back seat of a car in 1976 during the smugness of late July.

It is the perfect fall day for travelling and the plan is to get to the gathering point on the big lake to rest, visit with our relatives and wait for the thermoclines. The maples are radiating orange brazen hope burning away the night moisture. The sky is bright endless blue. The easy weather is a good sign, like maybe this isn't a mistake or an unnecessary risk.

The three old ones, siblings, out front, know the way. This is their twentieth, twenty-first and twenty-second trip, respectively. Their three families, both genetic and chosen, make up the rest of the squad. The sky brings out both the best and the worst of everyone, as it is with all families, but the three siblings are resolute in their commitment to this way of life, at least in front of the rest. Their quiet insecurities are kept among them in the angle between each arm of the formation.

Every year, fewer folks choose to make the journey and more choose to stay and become year-round residents. It is a different life for sure. For the siblings, the justifications of the residents fall short — it's less dangerous, it's a different time, a break from tradition, there's enough food so there is no need, the trip is just too demanding, it's too hard to take that much time off.

To the oldest sibling, Mandaminaakoog, these excuses can be summed up by one word: complacency. Mandaminaakoog cannot imagine life without movement, without the continuous work that brings about equal parts paralyzing exhaustion and the sweetness of uncomplicated fulfillment. Mandaminaakoog cannot imagine life without the task of one's existence being dependent upon continual remembering. Life as an economy of meaning. An actual good life.

Mashkodiisiminag and Kosimaanan are less sure, and less vocal. Mashkodiisiminag thinks less philosophically than Mandaminaakoog. They like the change of scenery and being in a different place every night. They like the freedom of flight, hours and hours of quiet. They like never being alone. They like the synergy of moving through waves of air like a body much larger than the sum of its parts. They like the accomplishment of being in a different place every night.

Kosimaanan is in it for the odd set of circumstances and the happenstance of travel. The poetry hidden in the space between left and leaving. The infusion of stories and joking pulsing through the formation. The time Nanabush came too. The time that crazy zhaganash took some resident tourists to Virginia in an ultralight. Kosimaanan will tell the stories at the right time, maybe at a gathering spot as the sun sets. Maybe when breast muscles are screaming and wings are numb with exertion. Maybe when corticosterone is as high as it gets and thyroid hormones have peaked. Maybe whispered between the sentinels at night when everyone else is asleep on the water. Maybe just to the first-timers at the back, the ones that never take the lead.

The night before they left, they sat in council with the residents. Mandaminaakoog resented the circle. This is supposed to be ceremony. This is supposed to be a celebration, not an ordeal; a coming together, not a dividing line between resident and migrant, between an old order and a new order that should not exist. A new order built on shortcuts and self-interest rather than service and excellence.

Mandaminaakoog knows that their resentment was not helpful. They know that unity is more important, they know that the ethic of influence is through action, not talking. But in their core they simply could not understand or respect the decision of the residents to stay, and they judge them. It is easy. It is lazy. It is the antithesis of their collective existence. The cost, the character of meaning. The silent sacrifice found in the quality of the weave, creating the very fabric of formation after formation.

By all accounts, this nation and all of our formations are doing well — one of the few expected to survive. We've learned to thrive in urban places humans have utterly ruined. We've adjusted our flight paths to avoid twenty-four hours of artificial light, planes and the windows of high-rises. Our medicines have contained H_5N_1. We've outrun culling, the salinity-induced mortality of our babies and new arrhythmic weather. We've witnessed the loss of so many of our relations. We've made flyways through the grief.

One could therefore go as far as to say this is a privileged conflict between residents and migrants, because first of all, it is a decision we have some control over, it isn't something that's been blindly done to us while the bodies piled up, like with buffalo or the caribou or the eel. This is precisely what pushes Mandaminaakoog's resentment into angry. It simply does not have to be this way. We could collectively choose different. Mandaminaakoog stores will in the hollow of their feathers. They release it through the flock after 750 miles at forty miles per hour. They fan it through wingspans until it falls back to aki and lands on the soil like seeds.

Shkaabewis understands all that, and that's why Shkaabewis is here instead of with their own family. It matters to them how they live. They need to have the lightning of adrenaline coded into their veins when the constellations shift and the time for preparing is done. They need to read time through thermoclines. They need to look down from three thousand metres above earth level.

Not everyone needs to do this.

Not everyone is lucky enough to find the thing that gives them purpose, and that makes most everything else seem meaningless.

Mandaminaakoog does not hold anger for very long. They remember it matters more that some are going than that some are staying. They sing the songs that map the route. They read the stars. They hold all the ones that have come before. They think about which young ones to rotate into the lead. They wonder which old ones have passed and won't make it to the gathering spot on the north side of the big lake.

SHKAABEWIS

The three siblings sleep until first light. They breathe light in, rouse us with gentle "ambe maajaadaa's", and then we take off from the river, encouraging each other, saying "until later" to the residents, love lifting our beating wings up.

MASHKODIISIMINAG

LECTURE ONE:

Mashkodiisiminag counsels the younger ones before the start date, primarily about bringing nothing. In the old days, there was nothing to bring, but the young resident geese are used to having things and keeping things and relying, well, on things. Mashkodiisiminag over and over says: "Pack it in your bones, find it along the way, and every thing gets left."

MASHKODIISIMINAG

LECTURE TWO:

Mashkodiisiminag counsels the younger ones on what to say out loud and what to put in their do-not-say bins. These ones are used to typing and posting every thought with few consequences and so Mashkodiisiminag is lecturing on thinking it through. Thinking of the formation above oneself. Think of everything that could possibly happen if you say "I hate the smell of Bezhig's ass feathers" out loud. Think of the ones that will laugh and feel affirmed, having followed Bezhig's ass across the continent. Think of the positive energy that generates. Think of the ones that will worry their ass feathers smell as well and who will look over their wing to the back of the formation the next chance they get and for a fraction of a second slow the whole thing down. Think of those that will feel irritated at the very sound of your voice for reasons you can't possibly know or predict. Think of those that have been taught to feel shame about their asses and their feathers and who have been robbed of their sovereignty around both. Think of Bezhig themselves and whether or not they have enough in their emotional reserve to ride out the teasing. Think about what kind of log the fire needs.

Think about why you feel the need to say it. Turn it in on yourself.

MASHKODIISIMINAG

LECTURE THREE:
"Don't think too much and don't worry too much."

Each year, the conversation requires more and more counsel and more and more support. There are those young ones that see it as the ultimate challenge and there are those that see it as a ridiculous and unnecessary throwback to something that might have served formations well in the past, but whose time has expired. There are squads that have ground support carrying things, and this makes it a different thing altogether. Folks pack books and nesting materials, favourite snacks and comfort items. *Things* to rely on.

Mandaminaakoog sees things differently. The practice of formation above all else. "Pack it in your bones, find it along the way, every *thing* gets left." The formation must find hope, faith and the wherewithal to continue. The formation must find it in themselves or the ones they meet along the way. They must nurture and find comfort. They must take care of the need of everyone in position all the time. They must practice being an ear of corn, not a kernel.

LECTURE FOUR:

By lecture four, Mashkodiisiminag has weeded most of the tourists out, or rather, the tourists have weeded themselves out, having properly assessed this mission as not the end-of-adolescence backpacking trip to Europe they were looking for. That's why this lecture is entitled "What to Do When You Hate Everyone around You and You're Stuck with Them for Several More Months."

LECTURE FIVE:

Lecture Five (which inevitably stems from the real-life failure of Lecture Four), is called "What to Do When You're Done and You No Longer See the Value in Migration, Your Peers, the Formation and Being a Goose." Kosimaanan rides the line between the value of figuring out something important about yourself and changing one's actions accordingly, and the real need to just continue the journey by any means. The act of not quitting. The practice of recognizing depletion in oneself and not getting tripped up by it. They teach the students, knowing that some will succumb anyway, to disconnect one's mind from those thoughts, speaking back to them and engaging in a singular focus. The failure of Lecture Five inevitably leads to Lecture Six.

LECTURE SIX:

Lecture Six is on performance-enhancing drugs, like caffeine and sparkly water and sugar and the internet. Mashkodiisiminag begins with the usual angle, "There are no performance-enhancing drugs that are useful on this journey, because it is too long and too real and the temporary benefits one might achieve through use will always pale in comparison to the consequence." It isn't that it is cheating. It is that cheating then transfers a bigger load of work to others in formation around you. It is that the formation pays for the individual benefit.

This is the most difficult of the conversations. It never goes well. Mashkodiisiminag always comes out feeling like a cult leader or worse. They find it nearly impossible to convince this next generation that playing with internal chemistry fucks it up. They find it nearly impossible to convince these goslings that it is important to train your neuropathways to cope with crisis, trauma and danger on their own. That feeling is something one must have sovereignty over. That this is a gift and an asset.

This is the biggest difference between resident and migratory life. This creates the judgements, the resentments, the authenticity debates, the debates around who is privileged and who is not.

LECTURE SEVEN:
Work harder than you thought possible.
Believe.
Sign the waiver.

The art of . . . well . . .

The art of getting to know someone.

Mashkodiisiminag takes the most hits amongst the residents. On summer nights, they gather in Tommy Thompson Park and recount the stories from the migration before. When they first get back, it is the most recent journey. By midsummer, it is the highlight reels of the past twenty-one journeys, mixed with the classics. When Minomiin Giizis appears, Mashkodiisiminag descends into formation theory, the history of flight and the first migration.

Kosimaanan's stories were also lectures, but sneak lectures so the youth of the flock thought it was entertainment, not education. The nightly gatherings were also supposed to strengthen the ties between the residents and the migrants, and the residents had their own history to tell. The practice of staying was also difficult. The practice of staying was also dangerous.

KOSIMAANAN

STORY ONE: ON WHY WE DO THIS, ANYWAY

Long, long time ago birds didn't migrate. We were one of many nations in formation under one sky. But then there was a fight because there is always a fight. It matters not what the fight was about but in this case let's say it was somewhat legitimate in that there simply wasn't enough food to support all the residents even though the white people had yet to come here and fuck absolutely everything up. We split into two teams. Sometimes people say birds versus animals some people say birds versus birds. I'm saying birds versus birds because that carries more meaning for an all-goose audience. A lacrosse game. And now the losers, or the winners, depending upon perspective, fly south in the fall, all the way to Florida, and then north in the spring, all the way to not-Florida. You'd think after founding a cult and holding lectures and all the governance and logistics meetings and all the sermons about faith and excellence and commitment, we'd get someplace better than Florida. The guns. The old whites. The flip-flops. The humidity.

STORY TWO: ON WHY WE DON'T TAKE TOURISTS WITH US

Oh of course Nanabush begged and begged to come. And of course we resisted and resisted until they drove us goddamn crazy nuts and it was easier to just carry them all the way to Florida in formation than listen to one more second of begging. We gave them rules, primarily to preserve what was left of our own sanity, and they broke them. We were compassionate and then we weren't and we dropped them and that was that. No more tourists.

STORY THREE: THE HUMBLE ORIGINS OF THE V-FORMATION

OK. Ok. ok. Okay.

Nahow.

Nanabush Part Two . . . feeling lazy, hungry, yep. Yep. Sees some geese out resting on the lake. Just sitting there. Makes a rope out of cedar bark, swims out with snorkels and fins and ties a few legs of the geese with the rope. It's going so good and easy with the full-mask deluxe snorkel that they decide to tie up all the geese. Gets over-excited. Gets water in their snorkel. Chokes a bit. Causes a commotion. Scares the geese and they FLY, because they can, and while they're flying with their legs tied together in a V, they notice it's easier. So they cut that rope and kept on doing it, because everyone knows geese love PHYSICS.

STORY FOUR: ZHAGANASH AND THE ULTRALIGHT, OR ON NOT
KNOWING YOUR PLACE

FFS, the best allies are really those ones that stay in their own lane
and don't try to help. This friggen zhaganash builds a plane and gets
these poor scooped-up goslings to imprint on them and they fly them
to Florida and drop them off in a field and what in the actual fuck
are we supposed to do with them now? Not to mention that we had
already organized our own formations to pick a few of them up but
that goddamn ultralight nutbar got there first.

KOSIMAANAN

STORY FIVE: A SHORT HISTORY OF THE INDIANS OF CANADA

Mashkodiisiminag begins by saying that they learned this story from Thomas King and that it is not their story by any means.

KOSIMAANAN

STORY SIX: OMIIMIIG

One time not that long ago the omiimiig filled the sky over the lakes in mid-afternoon. Name the lakes. So many omiimiig that the sky went dark.

KOSIMAANAN

Some stories are stories and some are just facts, facts so important that story can't mess with them.

STORY SEVEN: PINK GULL

*Note: The Gull wasn't really a gull, but the identity of the bird in question has been changed to protect the innocent.

The One Who Stayed told this one the best. They were on a motivational speaking tour making a stop in Yellowknife in the fall. The migrants were already moving and the bird activity was substantial at the airport. The One Who Stayed refrained from taking their tray table out of the locked position during takeoff. The One Who Stayed refrained from lowering their seat back to the reclined position during takeoff. The One Who Stayed begrudgingly removed their headphones for takeoff, staring out the window as the Bombardier CRJ900 sped towards liftoff, stymied only by the Gull that flew into the left engine producing a thump and then a soft, pink mist.

ASIN

Asin notices they gather just after the sun has set, so slightly later every day, noticeably later every few weeks. They can see that one of the older ones does most of the communicating, and at first Asin believes they are upset about something, or grieving, perhaps. Over time, they recognize calmness in the spoken words. Asin takes notes about this one first.

ASIN

Asin arrives at the lake with Biidaaban. It's fall and it's too hot. Asin needs a tank top, a wide-brim hat and copious amounts of sunscreen, not jeans, a hoodie and a beanie. Biidaaban is dressed more appropriately but it is easy for them. They mostly live here.

They can see the stalks on the lake near the shore, filling the bay with prairie. That's a good sign. At least they can see the stalks of rice.

They'll have to borrow the lawn of a cottage to get down to the water and launch the canoe, then paddle over to the bay and see if the grains are ripe or already planted in the substrate of the lake.

Biidaaban in the stern, Asin in the front. It takes a minute to fall into the rhythm of working together, to get the canoe to track straight and paddle across the lake to the far side, where the ducks and geese are gathered. When they arrive, Asin turns around, takes the cedar sticks and begins to knock the rice gently onto the Certified Value Tarps 15 × 20 in royal blue that Mindimooyenh gave them and which are spread out on the bottom of the canoe.

ASIN

After a few hours, they have a tiny pile of grains, bugs and leaves.

ASIN

After a few more hours, the pile grows, but it is nothing to brag about.

After a few more hours, Biidaaban comments that the storm last weekend must have knocked a lot of grains off the stock. You almost have to live beside the rice to catch it, they say.

By the time they start to lose the sun, they have enough, or at least Asin thinks so. They bundle it up in the Certified Value Tarps 15 × 20 in royal blue. Biidaaban asks why they are taking their pile back to the city instead of soaking it overnight, drying it and then parching. Asin smiles.

Asin and Biidaaban drive into the big city beside the big lake and go directly to Tommy Thompson Park. They park the car, put on their headlamps and hike to the geese's staging ground with the Certified Value Tarps 15 × 20 in royal blue. In the stopping part of the night, they spread the Certified Value Tarps 15 × 20 in royal blue with the grains out where the geese are sure to find them first thing. Biidaaban lies down on their side in the grass a distance back. Asin lies down in the grass too, beside Biidaaban.

Biidaaban thinks carefully about how to make this happen.

Weweni.

Thinks it through in seven directions.

Thinks it first, before attempting execution.

And then Biidaaban closes the space between Asin's body and theirs, fits Asin's body into Biidaaban's. Biidaaban's brown warmth holding the ancient rock, their finger circling on Asin's arm. They face the Certified Value Tarps 15 × 20 in royal blue and fall asleep, waiting to see the look of their faces.

TEN

DEGENTRIFICATION

ADIK

Adik took off their backpack for the first time in three days. They paid attention to the sound of the broken brown leaves, and the smell of the lake and the dark. They looked up and then around for the moon. They sighed.

ADIK

Adik had been visiting for most of the night. Handing out, with Ninaatig, sleeping bags, naloxone kits, soup and stories to the Nishnaabeg-that-stayed. Smudging off those that needed medicine. Rubbing sore and tired feet and backs as requested. Ninaatig kept the soup in their shopping cart. The sleeping bags were cached in hide-lined pits throughout the city, and most of the Nishnaabeg-that-stayed knew where they were located. Adik and Ninaatig had worked tirelessly for a decade to set up this network, map it out and code it.

ESIBAN

Esibanag dug caches throughout the city in parks where they stored the essentials:

naloxone kits

sleeping bags

dry caribou meat from the Dene

only the kindest of words

You know the Nishnaabeg-that-stayed as the homeless. The ones we are all related to. The forgotten ones. The ones that we think need *help*, but we don't help. The only ones not on Twitter, Facebook and Instagram.

Esibanag know them as the Unceded Nation Under the Gardiner. In tents and tarps. Checking in. Visiting. Taking care the best they can. Using whatever they find. Taking only what they need. Sharing everything they have. My heart.

GIDIGAA BIZHIW

Gidigaa Bizhiw drew maps on the sides of buildings with stencils and green spray paint. It wasn't a perfect system, but it was a coordinated system of secret care, hidden under the guise of homeless, pest, defeated and indifferent.

GIDIGAA BIZHIW

One might describe Gidigaa Bizhiw as awkward.

GIDIGAA BIZHIW

Painfully introverted.

GIDIGAA BIZHIW

Incapable of the small talking.

GIDIGAA BIZHIW

Gidigaa Bizhiw prefers misunderstood, mysterious, shy even. Extinct.

GIDIGAA BIZHIW

stencils
green paint
speed
a hemisphere of trees

GIDIGAA BIZHIW

they spray
white pines
cedar
maples
on steel
concrete
brick
white picket fences
pressure-treated back decks
and the blue light of screens

GIDIGAA BIZHIW

*and a plastic wading pool

**and the green bin with the chicken wings beside the plastic wading pool

***and the word "ARTIST" on Bougie Kwe's garage door so Bougie Kwe could take a selfie and post it on Instagram and Gidigaa Bizhiw would be also digital.

over time they forget the details.

GIDIGAA BIZHIW

over time, the flatness of cedar becomes round.

over time, they forget that softwoods make breath out of light and soft out of sharp edges.

GIDIGAA BIZHIW

they spray
white pines
cedar
maples
on steel
concrete
brick
white picket fences
pressure-treated back decks
and the blue light of screens

GIDIGAA BIZHIW

stencils
green paint
speed
and a hemisphere of trees

The Esibanag were the ultimate radicals and no one knew it. Sure, they had been dispossessed, displaced and their habitat gentrified like everyone else, but they were not taking it. No way. They moved the fuck back in. Committed. Built lodges, spoke their language, did their ceremonies and took care of each other. They had kids and more kids and raised them up to be self-determining fire. They figured out how to live with the asshat humans in harmony such that the biggest asshat human complaint was that they had to clean up their garbage every few days.

ESIBAN

Esiban important practice number one: Don't leave. No matter what.

Esibanag moved back in, and then learned all kinds of new shit like how to break zip-ties and open the green bins and the new, extra-expensive green bins, and how to do public relations. They learned to tilt their heads at the cameras to look omg so cute. They learned to parade out their babies in a line, ride the subway and steal donuts. They learned how to do the odd well-timed comedic adventure like falling through a skylight or staging a hilarious home invasion or drinking Coke right out of the can or posing for Instagram photos. They staged their own memorials when one of them died, with cheap roses and teddy bears. They signed the scientists' consent forms and got SSHRC and NSERC funding and got their blood pressure taken and their weight recorded. They listened earnestly to the lectures about over-eating and exercise and smoking. They learned about distemper and diabetes. They learned the importance of presence — showing up at kid soccer games; being overly nice to dogs; and the ultimate, getting spit out onto the baggage carousel at Pearson to cheer those of us that had reached the end of our ropes waiting in lineups, watching shit movies and eating Italian wedding soup like it was going out of style. They dug outhouses and undid zippers and mason jars and made headlines with their raccoon brilliance. "Trash Pandas: Smarter than cats and white rats — with the intelligence of a human toddler!"

Esiban important practice number two: Act like you are supposed to be there.

MINDIMOOYENH

We are supposed to eat raccoons, FFS.

MINDIMOOYENH

Cooked right, they are tasty, FFS.

MINDIMOOYENH

Raccoons never line up for brunch.

BOUGIE KWE

#urbankwe #bougie

Bougie Kwe decided to classy the joint up a bit.

BOUGIE KWE

With a Zen meditation pond in the backyard.

Made out of a plastic wading pool from Canadian Tire that they tied to the roof of an Uber to get home.

Esibanag just watched and watched. First the four $46.99 water lilies planted, one for each direction. Then the rocks repurposed from Ward's Island. Then the bags of rocks and gravel and mud as substrate. The carefully positioned leaves.

The pièce de résistance: floating hyacinths.

Bougie Kwe googled:

"Beautiful but destructive in the wrong environment, water hyacinths (*Eichhornia crassipes*) are among the showiest of water garden plants. Flower stalks that grow about six inches above the foliage arise from the centers of the rosettes in spring, and by the end of spring, each plant holds as many as 20 gorgeous purple flowers."

Read more on the internet at *Gardening Know How* ("Tips for Growing Water Hyacinth Plants").

BOUGIE KWE

Bougie Kwe googled:

"Nimaamaa ko ogii-nookizwaan iniw esibanan."

BOUGIE KWE

You can make fun of Bougie Kwe all you want, but they are just doing what every other NDN in the city is trying to do, which is not end it all, by bringing a little bit of real right into the city. Pumpkin seeds in "repurposed" Styrofoam coffee cups. Trilliums in the garden. Fires in the backyard. Hyacinths in a plastic wading pool. Semaa at the base of street lights. Duck soup Under the Gardiner.

BOUGIE KWE

It was finally finished.

ESIBAN

It was finally finished.

The first night, Esibanag really couldn't believe their eyes and luck and good fortune. The cool water. The water lilies. The floating hyacinths. The rocks. Brought back the memory of foraging for food along the shore. Brought back the whole washing-their-food debate.

Emerged.

ESIBAN

Floating.

ESIBAN

Surrounded by hyacinths and moonlight.

ESIBAN

Drinking the cool night water in, and then out.

ESIBAN

It was unreal for the first week. A secret night spa at 10 p.m. Diet Coke and chocolate and alone-Netflix. A treat just for Esiban. Glorious, indulgent me time. Then, gradually, word got out. More and more people came. Things got out of hand a bit with all the excitement. One thing, inevitably, led to another.

Esiban important practice number three: Make the very, very best of things.

BOUGIE KWE

Ripped-up water lilies.

BOUGIE KWE

Rocks all tossed.

BOUGIE KWE

Floating hyacinths, trashed.

BOUGIE KWE

Bougie Kwe hip-hopping mad.

BOUGIE KWE

Regrouping.

Refusing.

BOUGIE KWE

Rebuilt.

Bougie Kwe rebuilt four times, one for each of the sacred directions. Then the Lee Valley catalogue arrived at the front door because *Bougie* Kwe, and who doesn't like a posh garden tool. On page 34 was a Raccoon-Sensing Spray Blaster, which was really called the Pest-Deterring Jet Sprayer, for $59.50 plus shipping. Bougie Kwe indulged. With express shipping it arrived in two days and was immediately installed.

Esiban could not believe their eyes. Now the pièce de résistance had a new pièce de résistance and it was a fountain. Glorious. While the alone-time spa party was over, the community pond party was not.

Bougie Kwe did not give up. Not initially, anyway. They would set the Pest-Deterring Jet Sprayer and hide and wait, and then set the Pest-Deterring Jet Sprayer and wait and hide again. Mostly, though, they would forget it was running and scare the shit out of themselves when it suddenly fired up and blasted water at them when they were picking organic local hand-picked-by-the-eastern-woodland-bougie-NDN lettuce.

Which brings us to lettuce and prize-winning heirloom tomatoes falling off the vine that would win prizes if anyone still cared about that sort of thing.

Tomatoes on the vine, ripe with antioxidants you don't even know the likes of, and Esibanag march right past them every night at the pond party and goes for the college kid's green bin to find chicken wings.

BOUGIE KWE

Diabetes is a choice, if you forget colonialism, fellas. Bougie Kwe most certainly provided tomatoes and lettuce.

Consumption guidelines for not getting diabetes (according to Wikipedia):

40% invertebrates
33% plants
27% vertebrates

Results of the garbage-bin consumption study completed in 2019:

40% chicken wings
33% not-that-rotten fruits and vegetables from California
27% straws

Esiban assembled the crew at 12:15 a.m. because it was going to take most of the night.

ESIBAN

Esiban divided the volunteers into four groups and ordered four Ubers, ten minutes apart:

rocks
pool
plants
healthy hors d'oeuvres

There were four in each group and Esiban enjoyed the symmetry of it all.

When the final bag of organic lettuce and heirloom tomatoes arrived in the Uber at the Unceded Nation Under the Gardiner, everyone was there. Ninaatig all proud. Adik all interested and slightly confused but willing to move out of their comfort zone. Nishnaabeg-that-stayed ready for a celebration.

BOUGIE KWE

Bougie Kwe Ubered down to the Unceded Nation Under the Gardiner with their hunting knife, a big pot and the eighteen-pound bone-in ham they won at the not-super Superstore for spending over $200.

ASIN

Asin showed up with half a cup of minomiin that tasted like the lake.

ADIK

Adik showed up with a backpack full of naloxone kits.

NINAATIG

Ninaatig showed up with their shopping cart full of supplies.

GIDIGAA BIZHIW

Gidigaa Bizhiw showed up twelve hours early and decorated.

ESIBAN

Each group installed their responsibility:

rocks
plastic pool
water lilies and floating hyacinth
green bins full of lettuce and heirloom tomatoes

And they took turns running through the Pest-Deterring Jet Sprayer,
which retails for $59.50 at Lee Valley.

Esiban important practice number four: Take very, very good care of each other, always, no matter what happens.

The geese fly overhead in the sheer grace of a carefully angled formation designed to take them elsewhere.

There are still stars.

There are still stars.

KIMIIGWECHIWII'ININIM

Miigwech to Ansley and Shannon Simpson for lending me some of their stories, to Minowewebeneshiinh Simpson for her research and knowledge of the boreal owl, to Nick Ferrio for sharing his "pink mist" experience with me, to Madeline Whetung for sharing the phrase from her Grandfather, "You think too much you worry too much," and to Doug Williams whose never-ending influence is everywhere. Thanks to Sarah MacLachlan, Janie Yoon, Melanie Little, Maria Golikova and the entire team at House of Anansi Press for their collective care, vision, trust and book-making magic. Thanks to Marilyn Biderman at Transatlantic for spinning the dials.

Damian Rogers sharpened the execution and the intervention of this book in a way that few could have. She lived inside this book for countless hours, thinking through pronouns, tenses, voice, and offering valuable insights into this world and the characters that make it. She engaged carefully, thoroughly and with all of her spirit, emotions, intellect and physicality and I am ever so grateful.

The title "Noopiming: The Cure for White Ladies" was motivated by Susanna Moodie's *Roughing It in the Bush*, published in 1852. Doug Williams tells me that Michi Saagiig Nishnaabe pronounce it as "nookiming"; the more standard spelling is used in the title.

The Fred Moten epigraph appearing at the beginning of this book is from the talk "The Black Outdoors: Saidiya Hartman and Fred Moten with J. Kameron Carter and Sarah Jane Cervenak" at Duke University, September 23, 2016.

"Thinking rethinking, thinking otherwise," "gathering into gatherings," and "useful uselessness of despair" are all from Kodwo

Eshun's Mark Fisher Memorial Lecture at Goldsmiths, University of London, January 19, 2018.

"Hello my friend, I've come to see you again" is from Gord Downie's "The East Wind' off the record *The Grand Bounce* (Universal Music Canada, 2010).

"Mobilization of Joy," "practice of joy," and "protection of joy" are concepts from the work of Robin D. G. Kelley.

I consulted various web-based articles on the research of York University's Suzanne MacDonald into raccoons, including "Humans and Raccoons Can Coexist in Cities" (Laura Sciarpelletti, CBC News, August 6, 2018), "Toronto built a better green bin and — oops — maybe a smarter raccoon" (Amy Dempsey, *Toronto Star,* August 30, 2018), and "There's No Stopping Toronto's 'Uber-Raccoon'" (NPR, September 16, 2018).

Chi'miigwech to the Ojibwe People's Dictionary for their presence on the internet.

"death by water" was previously published by *The Walrus;* "failure of melting" and "head of the lake" were previously published by *West End Phoenix;* "viscosity" and "head of the lake" were previously published by *Five Dials.*

Some of the poetry in "theory of ice" has been adapted for a forthcoming album of the same name.

LEANNE BETASAMOSAKE SIMPSON is a Michi Saagiig Nishnaabeg writer, scholar, and musician, and is a member of Alderville First Nation. She is the author of seven books, including *This Accident of Being Lost*, which won the MacEwan University Book of the Year; was a finalist for the Rogers Writers' Trust Fiction Prize and the Trillium Book Award; was longlisted for CBC Canada Reads; and was named a best book of the year by the *Globe and Mail*, the *National Post*, and *Quill & Quire*. She has released three albums, including *f(l)ight*, which is a companion piece to *This Accident of Being Lost*.